This Christmas in Love

TIFFANY BLACK

ISBN: 979-8-9938327-1-5

DEDICATION

It's weird to dedicate a book with love scenes to my mom and aunts so the *effort* required to produce this book is dedicated to my mother and aunties: The first 'book club' I ever witnessed. I love you all and thank you for being an infinite inspiration of love for me.

CONTENTS

ACKNOWLEDGMENTS

This book was born out of my love for writing and the frustration with how stifled the entertainment industry has become. Creators create. Writers write. And I still believe in a good story.

To my ride-or-dies — thank you for standing with me in faith, for encouraging me when I forget who I am, and for reminding me to write the story I wanted to read.

To my creative tribe — the actors, writers, and dreamers who inspire me daily — your brilliance keeps me honest.

To every reader who picked up this book — thank you. You make it possible for stories like this to exist. My hope is that *This Christmas in Love* reminds you that love is worth believing in.

CHAPTER 1

I stood there looking at this beautiful man I had come to love. He stood an entire foot taller than me and had always been a toasted light-skinned Adonis mountain I loved to climb. Juke was so big in stature, I could lie on top of him and never touch the bed. If I sat on his lap, my feet never touched the floor. He opened doors for me from behind. He was the epitome of a protector, but the flip side of that was that he could cast a shadow of darkness over me.

I had been loving Juke for a long time. And sure, today he's an NFL player but it was me doing his homework in college that kept him on the field when the university almost kicked him out for failing his classes. This wasn't uncommon behavior. We went to a D1 school and even though we were more off than on during college, because he couldn't keep his pants around his waist, I knew he needed me. I knew that point in his life would pass. And I knew when he was done falling for cheap, easy sex, he'd come back home. Which he did. Juke got drafted during our junior year in college. We had already broken up by that point but I was happy for him. I loved him. We were friends. When I graduated and attended NYU to earn my MBA, he soon got traded to the team in New York. He considered it fate. We got back together like no time had passed. Life was busy but nights were cozy. I was able to make it to class and back to our posh loft apartment in Manhattan late in the afternoon. I prided myself on keeping a clean home and having food on the stove by the time he got in from practice. When I graduated, I only took jobs in the city so I could be front and center at home games and down to ride for his away games. I knew how thirsty women could be and I would be damned if I wasn't in arms reach when my man was looking for me.

It took a lot of sacrifice for my professional life but I worked triple and double time during the week so I could be there for him when he needed me. I got so sick of my career suffering because I was chasing his that I finally decided to open my own firm offering brand management for companies so I could be my own boss and be on my own schedule. The clients kept coming. My work kept growing. I hired some friends to lighten my load and when I finally felt like I had a groove, consistent retainers, and a little bit of balance, Juke sprung a revelation on me that I just didn't see coming.

With my two bachelors, earned simultaneously, including my MBA, I couldn't figure out how after years of loving, dating, and exclusivity, which doesn't include the years in high school and the on-and-off time during college, could I figure out how he arrived at the conclusion that he wasn't ready to get married.

THE FUCK.

"I'm just not ready. I still feel like we both have a lot to learn about ourselves and each other. I could get traded next year and you built your whole company around New York. I can't ask you to move with me." Juke said as he towered over me.

I scratched my fresh sew-in. I could suddenly feel every stitch, every braid. It was tight around my edges. I tried to breathe deeply but the walls were closing in fast. My body was hot. I could feel the sweat under my arms creeping through my shirt. I hated when that happened. I searched for words.

"You could ask whatever you want of me if you'd asked me to marry you." I replied as calmly as I could muster.

"Sydni. I love you. I just don't think it's fair to propose just because you're ready and I'm not," He said.

"How could you not be ready? You've been with me more than you been with yourself since you were 17- Juke. This is blowing me," I spat back.

I could see I was making him uncomfortable. Until this moment I had completely forgotten that we were at one of his teammate's wedding receptions. They were already asking if we were next but me catching the bouquet helped nothing. I overheard him telling someone 'No time soon' as it pertained to marrying me and I flew off the handles. I had been keeping my French manicure immaculate expecting a ring any day now. For the last two years.

People walked by. We both faked smiles until they cleared. I saw the bride bustling her gown as she backed it up on her new husband. I was jealous. Embarrassed. Furious. This was our third wedding this year alone and we had been together longer than any of the couples jumping the broom. The good thing was that I had options: I could make a scene and embarrass us both. I could submit and continue to follow him to hell wasting what was left of my childbearing years. Or, I could fight back.

He pulled me in close by the small of my back. I breathed deeply, closing my eyes, releasing a tear I didn't know was there.

"Maybe we should just take a break," he whispered.

I laughed knowing not a damn thing was funny. This was typical Juke behavior: suggest a break so we could miss each other, he could smash whoever was in his comment section, and then come back to me and pick up where we left off. I wasn't doing that again. I looked at the diamonds on my wrist. I touched the matching tennis necklace around my neck. I thought about the four-bedroom penthouse New York apartment I had decorated with pieces from Restoration House. I thought about my Range Rover and the crystals on its handles and how I didn't even know where it was parked because concierge covers that when I whip into the building. I saw my large Chanel flap bag on wedding guest table #12. I thought about all I'd be leaving, which is more than enough to keep the average woman kept and quiet.

I started to second guess myself. Maybe I shouldn't pressure him for marriage. Married people get divorced all the time, it doesn't guarantee anything. I know Juke loves me. He shows me every day. So why was I pushing for a piece of paper? Why did this validation mean so much me? Who was I validating? Myself or others? If I was honest with myself, me and Juke had been together for so long I had developed embarrassment around being with him and not having a ring. It made me feel like I wasn't enough. And it made me feel uncertain and unsure. I wanted more from him and I felt like I didn't just deserve it. I had earned it. Then I remembered that I could not control the next phase of this relationship or him. This man had given me everything but his heart and I knew if I didn't ask for his love in blood, I'd never get it.

"No. No more breaks. I love you, Juke. And if you're still unsure about me and us being together, I'm done. We're either getting married or it's over. Forever this time," I stood on business.

He looked at me in disbelief. I had never said anything like that to him before but he knew I was serious. The air was thick. Everybody in the building was having a good time except us.

"Well I guess it's over," he said as he loosened his tie and returned to his friends. I stood motionless. Children running by me with baskets of flowers. I had a mind to cry but I had done enough of that. I assured myself I'd be alright.

Then I got a text. I looked at my phone, it was Juke: *No one is ever gonna love you more than me.*

And without saying goodbye, I left the party.

I don't know if it was colder outside or inside our New York penthouse. It was appropriately gloomy. Juke had an away game which meant I could pack and mourn without him. I was determined to be out by the time he got home.

The doorbell sounded.

I was expecting her so I left the door unlocked.

"It's open." I yelled.

In walked my best friend, Liza. We met in the 7th grade at PE and to this day she's still the funniest person I know. She wore the cutest cream catsuit with a matching hooded fur vest showing off her petite frame. She rocked a bald head like no one could. But with her flawless skin, juicy earrings and mink lash extensions, I didn't miss the hair.

I started shooting orders before she could even get inside good, "If you pack what I put pink stickers on, and I work own my closet, we could take a dinner break in about three hours and-."

She held up one hand to stop my presses. She slowly removed her oversized bug-eye shades as if she was already overwhelmed.

"I hope you don't mind, I hired some people." Liza said as she held the door open for five black men that were so big I knew they could lift me with one hand.

"Start with the pink stickers," Liza offered them as she grabbed my Hermes bag from the kitchen counter and me from the floor. "We're going to brunch. Now." I didn't have the energy to fight back so I followed her out my own door.

About 35 minutes later we were sitting inside a plastic bubble at a restaurant on the Manhattan side of the river. It was warm inside the bubble so we removed our fur. A waitress took our order, which was easy, because I didn't have an appetite. Liza listened as I recounted where I thought I made missteps. She let me vent about how angry I was at myself for what had not happened the way I imagined it would. She sat open, as I got it all out and then she looked at me.

"You done," she asked. I shook my head yes. "This is not your fault. You ain't did nothing but fall in love with a tall. light-skinned man. Honey, it happens to the best of us." And that offers me the release I hadn't felt in what feels like an eternity. Liza grabbed my hand across the table silently coaching me into repeating a mantra we hand be telling ourselves for years.

"Everything works out in my favor so this must be the biggest set up for true love in my entire life," I said. Liza agreed. Our lattes land on our table and we gently enter the next chapter.

CHAPTER 2

Three Months Later

The winter wind spanks my face. I raise a head nod to the folks on the block on the way into my office. My freshly styled, volumized bob sticks to my lip gloss. I look amazing, mainly because I refuse to look like what I've been through. Had it not been for the carolers outside my office building, I would not have known it was Christmastime.

I catch the latest ad placed outside my building for a dating app: *Bird in the Hand.* I would completely rework that ad, but that is not my client, and my plate is too full to fill it with hypothetical work.

Inside my office, it's clean, warm, and impeccably decorated. The rugs are plush. The art on the walls is saying something, and the phones are ringing, which means business is flowing as it should. I walk down the short hallway and into my private corner office, taking my seat by the window. I sit down and gaze at my trophies and plaques on the wall. I take in the images of me with celebs and business owners over the years. I roll my chair around to stare out at New York City. The only reason I built this company was to be able to give Juke my time without guilt, and somehow, I still landed on top. One thing a winner is gonna do- is win.

Liza comes switching into my office without knocking. There's no point—the walls and the doors are glass. Yes, Liza is my childhood best friend, but she also works for me. I know I can trust her to execute everything exactly how I like it, and she never takes it personally when I talk tough about business. Liza serves as my right hand and my rose-colored glasses. She's so optimistic about everything, I have literally witnessed her speak things into existence. She pulls ideas out of thin air and makes them real. She prays like an old church lady, and her faith makes me believe most things. Liza is the kind of person you want on your team—every team.

She's the one who came up with the idea to launch my own branding firm, and because she believed in me so much, she quit her job to work for me. For a while, I was paying her more than I paid myself. She's like a walking healing crystal. I'm lucky to have her.

"I've been doing some research, and according to the stages of grief, you're progressing unbelievably well," she says. I am completely confused. She knows this. "Stay with me. You need a subliminal personality test—so you can release control."

I agree to this, for no other reason than to humor myself. She tells me to close my eyes and imagine a room. In my mind, I see an empty, nondescript room I've never been inside. She tells me to find a box. So, I place a medium-sized cardboard box in the middle of the room. She tells me to find a ladder. I find this entire ordeal ridiculous. Like, why am I even doing this?

"Nothing about this is serious. Relax. There's a ladder somewhere in the room. Tell me when you see it," Liza says. I've never been good at hiding facial expressions. I smack my lips, find the ladder tall and against the wall. I shake my head yes, and she continues. She tells me there are flowers. I see three peonies on the windowsill and shake my head again. She tells me there's a horse. I throw my head back.

"Listen, you want some new results or not? You gotta let go sometimes. You need to understand why you're doing what you're doing in order to do something new. Now, let me know when you've found it," Liza barks at me.

Then I see a beautiful, brown, shiny horse with the most gorgeous mane and tail. He's in the room, off in the corner, facing the box. She tells me there's a storm.

"Inside the room?" I ask.

"You tell me," she says.

I see a storm outside the room. It's bad, but it's outside. I'm from Florida. I'm used to bad storms. They come and they go. No big deal.

"Okay, you can open your eyes. Do you want to know what all of this means?" Liza asks as if I haven't been begging for that the entire time.

She proceeds to tell me that the box represents me and my ego. If it's large, I have a big ego, and if it's small, I shrink myself for others. Mine was medium, so I took that to mean I'm perfect. I'm a Virgo, after all. God left us in charge.

She moves on to the ladder, which represents my ambition. When I told her, it was made of steel and went all the way to the ceiling, she told me I wasn't going to stop until I reached all of my dreams. That was not only true, but it was extremely affirming. I had been through a lot to get to where I was, and I was grateful that even in the days of feeling like I'd wasted years with a man, I still had my own money and my own career to stabilize me. I didn't have to wait on him to breadcrumb me to survive. Especially because girlfriends walk away with nothing, and only wives get half.

She continues with the flowers. Apparently, those represent how many children I want or how I like to be surrounded by friends and family. I definitely didn't want three kids—one was plenty for me. Then it was on to the horse. She asked questions about the horse before she told me what it meant. And when I told her it was beautiful, brown, standing facing the box, she said the horse represented my partner. I want him close, standing on business, and with his eyes on me. I loved that. It felt pretty accurate. The storm represents how I feel about adversity. And because the storm was bad but didn't shake me, she said I could handle anything.

"Where did you even learn this?" I asked her, masking how impressed I was with the accuracy.

She laughed, knowing I liked it, and told me she went on a first and last date with some guy at a coffee shop and he did the test on her. And just as I was about to indulge in overthinking it, my executive assistant saunters into my office. His name is Ryan. He's short, stocky, blonde, and gorgeous. I'm absolutely certain that he gets more facial treatments than I do, and he's still in his twenties. He's got his laptop in his hand, but he still summons us to the conference room to make his meeting official. Sometimes I think we work for him.

At the head of the conference table, he sits tall. He sweeps his pixie cut behind his ear, even though it was not in his face to begin with, and grins.

"I called this meeting this morning to inform you ladies of the happenings within Cole Standard, as owned by our CEO and Chief of Staff, Sydni Cole, and of course our Operating Manager, Liza Grant. Project overseen by myself, Ryan Davis," he says in the most unserious professional tone, which is completely unnecessary because the entire office is made up of us three and we've been working together for years.

"Ryan, get to the point," I interrupt him.

"Right. A car will be here to pick us up in fifteen minutes to transport us to the conference center for the Executive Fundraising Brunch," he says.

Me and Liza bust out laughing, because sir—it did not take all that. And we knew the car was coming because we scheduled it.

This is what made working with them so fun. Even when it was nothing, it was something.

Outside the conference hall, holiday lights sparkled across brownstones. Small families rush across the street bundled in coats. Breath is visible. Snow falls for the first time, encouraging children to capture the first taste.

Inside the conference hall was pandemonium. The room is bustling. Professional women greeted each other in the finest business attire and took their seats at tables so well decorated it looked more like a wedding reception—a far cry from the peace outside the doors.

At the center of it is me. Hair slicked back, wearing a stylish oversized men's suit with Vans.

I retreat to the bathroom to regroup. I wash my hands and dry them. I look in the mirror and take myself in. I pull an eye pencil out of my bag and perfect my eyebrow. I wet a finger and slick back an unruly sideburn.

Before leaving, I check myself from one side and then the other. I believe in looking the part, and I may or may not be obsessed with controlling every element of my life, but who doesn't want for things to go their way?

I return backstage, and Ryan hands me a blazer he finished steaming. My client, Mahalia Simpson—a smart woman in her sixties who usually has it together—enters looking a mess. My face must've looked like the *Scream* mask because Ryan quickly disappeared. I thought I was steaming the blazer to be helpful, but he was trying to piece Mahalia back together. She offered an explanation I didn't ask for.

"My daughter was supposed to do my hair, but my grandbaby got sick at school, so I did the best I could with it," Mahalia pleaded with me.

I wasn't pissed because she looked like Kentucky Fried Ass; I was pissed because I made her an appointment with one of the best stylists in Harlem, and she canceled it to save money by letting her daughter do it. If more women saw professional hairstyling as a true investment, they'd make more money. Anything that boosts your confidence and makes you show up more boldly in the world is worth the money. But Mahalia didn't see it that way. She thought she was saving money, when really, not getting her hair done was costing her money. I hated that for her.

I had her sit down and went to work on her hair. It was brittle and speckled with gray strands. Mahalia was due on stage in ten minutes, and I'm sorry, but we all know hair is the first thing everybody sees. Hair is where our confidence lies. I needed to save her speech so she could raise half a million in twenty minutes. I opted to slick her hair back into a sleek bun. I kept a lip-gloss-sized edge control in my purse for emergencies. I sent Liza to grab it. When she came back, panic was all over her face.

"What happened?" I begged her, still doing construction work on Mahalia's hair.

"Juke's here," she whispered.

"Why?" I shouted before I could control my fury.

"Oh, he's one of the sponsors for the event. Usually they just donate and don't come because it's a women's brunch, but we love Juke! He's got a table in the front!" Mahalia beamed.

I was annoyed. I kept wrestling with her hair as I watched him take pictures with the women, young and old. I could see the younger ones trying to press soft body parts up against him and the older ones trying to hook him up with their daughters. Typical man shit—they don't have to change; they just get to move on to a woman who doesn't know the truth yet.

We lock eyes.

Damn, he was fine.

It had been three months since I'd actually laid eyes on him, and he was finer than the wet dreams I still had about us. Juke gave Deion Sanders energy, and it was like Ginuwine's song *Pony* played every time I saw him again for the first time.

My pussy clenched. I swallowed hard, wondering if he knew he could have me back if he just came over and kissed me. My knees buckled, reminding me that he was no longer my man. I broke the eye contact and poured my attention into Mahalia. She used her phone as a mirror and was easily impressed with my instant hairstyling skills. I helped her into her blazer as Ryan came to whisper something to me.

"Your ex is over there," he said.

I told him I knew and to keep him away from me. Ryan left as quickly as he came.

"I put your speech notes on the podium. Go out there and raise $500k for your organization," I told Mahalia and took a deep breath.

Me and Liza watched her take the stage. I admired Mahalia so much. I knew I could never be the type of woman she was, but every time I worked with her, I was reminded how amazingly diverse Black women are. Mahalia was a chemist who created a neutralizing shampoo that restored hair fibers after they had been relaxed. She was actively working on a way to remove gel polish without it needing to be soaked or ruin the nail bed. The brunch was being held to raise money for research. Mahalia was filthy rich but still managed to look a mess herself. I could never understand, but this is part of the reason people paid me—for my taste.

Liza gets a text and quickly grabs her computer.

"It's Késha. She's on one again and—" Liza says, but I have to interrupt her.

"The mayor's daughter, Késha?" I ask.

Liza rolls her eyes while she pulls up a Zoom against my will. "Yes, Késha Sears. She's about to announce her parents' divorce tonight on her live podcast because Mayor Sears didn't buy her a G-Wagon for her birthday like she wanted. Go easy. You come for Késha, and you might be her next segment."

Liza offers me some earbuds and sends me on my way.

Késha has been one of my clients longer than I'm proud of. She's white, spoiled, and trying way too hard to be cool despite the fact that she's a constant embarrassment to her political family. Like, girl, all you gotta do is lean back and spend your daddy's money—but instead, she wants to pave her own way on uneven gravel to prove something to people who never gave a damn in the first place.

Mayor Sears first sought me because Késha wanted a singing career as a kid. It was during that time that I built a rapport with her that her parents, therapists, and boyfriends couldn't garner. I spoke her language. I saw the world just like her and was always able to get her to see it my way.

When she pops on the screen, I see her wrapping up an episode of her podcast. Her hot-pink podcast studio set looks like a life-size dollhouse, especially with her being a winter-white girl with platinum-blonde hair. Somehow, her North Star was always Black girl. Her branding, set, and fashion signal she's a powerful disruptor. I designed all of it.

Késha pops on, and her peppy attitude melts into ferocity. "My dad is a total embarrassment! He promised me he'd get me a G-Wagon so I wouldn't have to get a rich baby daddy!"

I remind her that we talked about this and warn her not to start acting a fool because it's almost time for her dad to run again. That wasn't enough, so I reminded her that there's nowhere to park in all of New York City, and if she pushes too hard for this G-Wagon, she may be forfeiting her driver. That got her off the ledge.

I shut the computer, signaling to Liza that I'd had another silent victory. "Hey, this is all good to go. I'm gonna head home," I tell Liza.

Liza approaches me to retrieve her laptop when her eyes get real big. When I turn around, I bump right into Juke. Great.

"Damn, you're beautiful," he says.

"I agree," I respond.

"Don't I look amazing?" he asks so genuinely you'd think the answer meant something.

"You got enough people telling you that, Juke," I shoot back.

"What's one more?" he asks. And with that, I'd had enough. I walk off. He follows me.

"I've been trying to call you, Syd," he says, demanding to lure me into an argument.

"You'll have to change your number to get through to me. Change. Something you promised to do and never did," I let the glass door slam in his face, but that didn't stop him from taking the scene outside.

"I'm sorry I hurt you," he says. And because I believed him, I stopped and turned to him.

"I'm sorry I kept giving you chances to," I respond.

"You really want to walk away from a high-quality man?" he says, letting me know he still thinks his status and money buy him the space to waste my time. I get all up in his face so he can feel my rage.

"You've been listening to too many podcasts. A high-value man is a man of his word. A high-value man can be trusted. A high-value man knows a high-value woman when he sees her—and when he does, he steps up. He makes her safe. He protects her heart. You, Juke Matthews, have a long way to go to become high value. Rich won't cut it."

My driver holds the door for me and closes it when I'm safely inside. Juke watches us pull away.

I made it back to my brownstone. It was still weird being back there, but I was grateful that I kept up with the mortgage despite being so sure of my spoiled life with Juke. I bought it back when I was working on my MBA and scraped together the mortgage by renting out the other floors and moving in my Aunt Vi as a roommate. I eventually convinced Juke it could become a rental property for us and he'd pitch in with maintenance.

Chaka Khan's voice greeted me before I finished climbing the stairs, along with the smell of curry shrimp, peas and rice, and cabbage. When I unlocked the door, Aunt Vi didn't even bother to turn around. She just ushered me over to the seven-foot Christmas tree she had meticulously decorated with a sheer white veil. The sight of it took my breath away. It was so beautiful and simple. Classic. Just like Aunt Vi. She saw me admiring the tree and climbed down her step stool.

I greeted her and proceeded with my night. I wasn't up for a fight, but I had asked her not to decorate the house for Christmas. I just wasn't in the mood, and New York during the holidays can be smothering enough. But Aunt Vi was a strong force, and she cared nothing about my desire to control things. As far as she was concerned, this had been her house for the last two years, and she would do exactly what she wanted with it.

I couldn't argue that. I also didn't plan on staying with her long. I just needed a soft place to land while I regrouped and got my thoughts together. I loved Aunt Vi. She'd never actually had to take care of me, but she definitely stepped in when my mother passed a month before my high school graduation. Aunt Vi has always been my surrogate, my voice of reason, my wise eye. Even when I didn't listen, it was nice to know there was someone who had me in their thoughts. Plus, she cooked.

She followed me into the kitchen, making me a plate. "Well, don't you like the tree?" she poked the bear.

"Auntie, you know how I feel about Christmas. It's a pagan holiday. I don't see the point, and it's bad enough that everyone else in this city is so captivated by lies and capitalism. I'm not, and it would be nice if you respected my wishes."

"At least I get to put a veil on something," she shot back.

This wasn't the conversation I wanted to have tonight. I really wanted to eat, shower, get in my bed, and go to sleep. But if I didn't check this and nip it in the bud, I knew it was only gonna get worse while I was crashing here. In my own damn house.

"With all due respect, that's a tree. I am a brand consultant. What I do is important. I fix people. I make them better. I protect them from themselves. And Christmas and/or a veil does not substantiate that or me. I—"

"Work too much," she said calmly, deescalating me instantly. She offered me the plate of food. Instead of taking it, I asked if Juke called her. She returned the same question. I told her if he does call, don't answer because I am done with him.

"You don't run me or this Motorola," she spat back. I thought for a second and responded.

"You don't trust who you helped raise?"

I was right. Aunt Vi, insulted, complimented, and defeated, backed off.

"I'll have you know I have a date tonight," I offered as a decline to dinner. With that, I left as fast as I'd come.

I waited outside Liza's call box, anticipating granted access. She finally comes down wearing an elegant short peignoir set. She was unpleasantly surprised to see me. I didn't care. She asked why I was there and why I was dressed up. I trailed her to her apartment.

"Why are you dressed like that?! I had to pretend I had a date to get my auntie out my business. I'm hiding out here because you don't have a man either," I said.

Once inside, I was ready to eat every word. I looked around: the lights were low, incense burned, and Liza was wearing a silk slip. It's definitely a vibe.

I asked, "Wait. Do you a man up in here?!"

"Not that I have to explain myself to you, but I become a woman after 8 p.m.," she said sheepishly.

I know. I'm just as lost as you are, because what does it even mean to become a woman after 8 p.m.? Were you not a woman before 8 p.m.?

This is the way she explained it: Becoming a woman at 8 p.m. means going feminine. Women work all day, and that has us in our masculine energy, but at 8 p.m., Liza chose to cut off the masculine and become a woman by not talking about work or even thinking about it. Instead, she focused on self-care, doing something she loves or doing nothing at all. And because our jobs are so demanding, carving out the time to relish in being a woman has to be intentional—or she'll just keep buying into the idea that we have to work twice as hard to be just as good, or the endless grind culture. Liza drew a line in the sand at 8 p.m.

All of that made sense to me. I wasn't about to be doing it because I'm about my money and my money can always reach me, but Liza? She was a girl's girl. Her only mission in life was to be loved, and she was going to make time for it even if it wasn't present yet.

"I'm a beast at 7:30 p.m. because my boss is a workhorse. But at 8 p.m., I am a woman. I bathe myself in Baccarat, I drape myself in silk, and I have dinner with my husband," she said boldly.

I looked around to make sure there wasn't a man present that I couldn't see, because I damn sure hadn't seen her walk down no aisle.

Liza had prepared a full dinner. She had a table set for two, which included a glass of red wine. If I didn't know any better, I'd think she was expecting me.

"He sits here. He hangs his coat next to mine. He drinks dry red," she continued with such clarity, I was looking for the mystery man's jacket!

She holds up an empty wine glass. I look at her in disbelief. Liza one-ups me and pours wine in it. I was outdone.

"You mean to tell me you waste wine every night on an invisible man?" Liza storms off back into the kitchen. I track her.

"I am making space for my husband. And in my marriage, we like to eat dinner together every night," she said.

I told her it was absurd. She told me it was faith.

I could sense that my pessimism wasn't welcomed here. And I could also sense that I wasn't welcome in my own home. And the truth was, I'd rather be with Liza. So, I decided to hear her out. Liza had been sleeping on one side of the bed, setting a table for two, and leaving a second toothbrush in her bathroom for months. I was hurt to learn that she wanted love so badly and felt like she couldn't share it with me. Even if I didn't believe in it, I would've helped her carry that dream. I apologized for making fun of her and assured her that I'd be holding space for her man in our lives too.

We enjoyed dinner, and I made it in late. I crept into the house, careful not to wake Aunt Vi, who fell asleep in her recliner, sewing a wig by hand. I take it out of her hand and cover her with a blanket.

Showered and in pajamas, I enter my bedroom wearing eye patches. I sprawl out in my bed and start scrolling on my phone. I have a dozen 'likes' from

Juke. On my latest post, he commented two rows of engagement ring emojis.

Then I get a text from an unsaved number: *Wyd.*

I text back: *Who is this?*

UNSAVED NUMBER: *Juke.*

I text back: *Sleep.*

I roll my eyes and close my phone. I lie there staring at the ceiling, thinking about Liza. I prayed that a man who loves her and who is completely emotionally available finds her and is intentional about building a life with her. Then I prayed for the space to even believe it could happen for me too.

I moved to one side of the bed, just to leave a little space for God to work a miracle.

CHAPTER 3

I whipped into my office, safe from the winter wind and snow flurries. My hair is bouncy and flowy just how I like it because I let my stylist cut as much as she wanted this time and didn't try to hold on to dead ends. Yeah, that's the vibe. No dead ends anywhere. I managed to find some Loewe wool trousers that had me thinking I was better than everybody else. My matching vest and monochromatic coat were the perfect touch. After all, the coat is the look.

I marched down the hallway like I owned it, because I did. I popped my head into the conference room where Ryan had unofficially made his headquarters. He used his computer camera to fix his hair. When I asked him what was going on, he said he was previewing a potential new client today.

"Anybody I should be excited about? You want me to sit in on it?" I asked, ready to roll up my sleeves.

"Well, it wouldn't be a preview meeting if you were in on it, now would it?" Ryan asked in a non-confrontational but territorial way.

I laughed, backing off. Ryan does a great job. He's got a bachelor's degree in my taste in clients. I backed off and opted to make a cup of coffee so I could hear a little bit of the call before retiring to my office.

Ryan launched the video call, and Evan Sterling popped on the screen. He's fit and well-dressed in a leisure suit. The brownstone he occupies is cozy and warm, filled with earth tones.

"Thanks for taking the time to have this preliminary meeting with me, Mr. Sterling," Ryan said, excited.

"No, thank you, Ryan," Evan asked, clarifying.

"That's right. I'm Miss Cole's executive assistant, and she likes to make sure all of our clients are a tonal match—and with this being in such short order…" Ryan handled himself with ease.

Evan got up and carried his computer with him, unintentionally exposing Ryan to more of his luxurious multi-story brownstone: imported stone, minimalist furniture, Black art, skyline, Baccarat glassware. Architectural Digest worthy.

From what I could see, Evan was fine—but more importantly, Ryan had everything covered.

Liza entered just in time to take the walk back with me. She's livid.

"Have you not seen this? Somebody recorded you and Juke arguing. It's all over the internet. Don't worry, I'm already on top of it. I've gotten a few sites to take it down, but Juke was also spotted out last night with another mystery woman, so that's fueling the fire," Liza went on without me even asking a question.

I was fuming, but I didn't want to hype her up any more than she already was. I knew that if I stayed grounded, she'd have to eventually match my energy. I sat at my desk and launched my own investigation while she continued.

"I just don't understand Juke. What was the point of coming to your client's event? He knew you were gonna be there because you're the reason he even donated to the cause. And while he's supposed to be trying to get you back, he's secretly taking up time with some random girl? Is that supposed to get you back? I was really holding out hope for him, but he is blowing this for me," Liza blew off steam.

I found the pictures of Juke and the girl. She didn't look familiar. He didn't look like he loved her. It looked like a means to an end. It still didn't feel good. It felt like a mess I'd already opted out of.

"Why aren't you saying anything?" Liza asked.

"What is there to say? Juke is not my man. And there's no point in getting worked up over a situation I already left because it wasn't serving me. I will say that I don't like being recorded without my consent, and I'd like you to secure an attorney. These people are messing with my brand. I refuse to have my likeness roped into the hell Juke's brand is headed toward without a wife and kids," I offered.

And with that, I moved on to my next task. Liza, amazed at my continued ability to compartmentalize, had no choice but to move on. She agreed to secure an attorney. She also informed me that the mayor's office sent my monthly retainer, Mahalia surpassed her goal, and asked if I'd decided to take on the new client.

"Evan Sterling? I think you should, Syd. He's a high-profile client who wants to work through the holidays. Came through some of our colleagues. Black tech billionaire. He needs an image reframe to save his dating app. I'm thinking a New Year's gala—bring people together to speed-date and find love just in time for the new year?"

Some colleagues contacted Liza about working through the holidays, and because she knows I'm not geeked out on Christmas, she thought it'd be a good project for me. She also mentioned that she would not be available to help me with this because, *"I'm going on vacation with my man."*

Ryan was confused. I told him I'd explain it all later.

"And the best part is that he's fine. Let's just say if he played for my team, he'd end the draft. Some people who met on his app had a tiff and blamed him. Subscribers are fleeting. Super unfortunate for him, but this could be extremely lucrative for us," Ryan raved.

Liza went on to explain that Evan escapes to his New Jersey mansion for Christmas annually and he'd like to work out there to avoid distractions. I launched a new investigation and found Evan's articles in *The Times, Forbes,* and *Fast Company*. One of his arms was the size of my torso. That got me a little moist. With a couple of strokes on my keyboard, I saw that he'd also never been married, had no kids, and was deep into his forties. He had a full hairline and just enough salt and pepper in his beard to tickle my kitty while he ate me for dessert. I licked my lips and turned back to my cohorts, resolved.

"Sounds like my kinda client. Ryan, I'll look at the contract, and Liza, I'll take the train. This sounds like the perfect escape and a great way to leverage our success with apps to garner new clients into the new year," I said.

"And he's rich and fine," Liza reminded me.

"He is wealthy and handsome, but I am a professional. Let's get this money."

Ryan and Liza exchanged a knowing look. I didn't feed it.

"Wait! We never discussed Juke popping up at the event to get you back! Any chance of a reconciliation?" Ryan asked with hopeful eyes.

"Absolutely not. I am not interested in getting back with Juke. I've given him enough of my childbearing years. He said he wasn't ready. We've been back and forth about this so many times—I'm done," I said, sure of myself.

Before they could question my sincerity, Liza had found me a ticket.

"I can get you out on the 8 a.m. train first thing in the morning," she said. I agreed to that, and I was on to the next task. My phone buzzed. I looked, and it was a text from the unsaved number—in other words, Juke.

UNKNOWN NUMBER: *Spend Christmas with me. We can go anywhere you want. I just want you with me.*

I shook my head in disbelief. I handed the phone to Liza and Ryan. Liza wanted to cuss him out. Ryan suggested I make him fly me private to Iceland. I decided to say nothing. I'd realized that silence is so much more puzzling than telling somebody what they already know. Juke knows he was having unprotected sex with a girl he barely knows last night. I don't need to tell him that. And I don't need to spend Christmas with him with that in the back of my mind. Why put myself through it? Why go back and forth? I don't need him to pick me over that because if he was really choosing me, he'd come with carats, not flights.

"Guess I'm headed to New Jersey," I said as I shut my laptop and gathered my things.

I folded my clothes and put them in a small carry-on suitcase. Aunt Vi invited herself in carrying a plate of freshly baked cookies. I couldn't tell if she wanted me to stay or if she was happy I'd be alone working with a rich man for the holidays. Something told me she was willing to be lonely to get me married off.

I enjoyed my auntie, but I often wondered what the hell she did in this house before I moved back in with her. She was married for a long time to my Uncle Francis. He passed away around eight years ago, and I never really saw her with another man. He was a good uncle, but I can't really say if he was a good husband. As I get older, I realize the two are very different. I can say that I never heard about any secret kids or other families coming out when he passed. My auntie never looked stressed, and while I do pay my own mortgage, she doesn't ask me for any money. I always assumed he took care of her in life and death. I could only respect a man who took care of home.

"Niece, listen to me. I'm not saying put yourself in a situation. I'm just saying if you get there and you like the man, enjoy him. Let him do the things he offers to do," she said.

I said nothing, hoping that if I didn't engage, she'd leave me alone. That did not work.

"Get your work done. But after that, if you can talk to him, and you can relate to him, open up, baby. Show him your heart," she said.

She offered me the tray of cookies.

"Auntie, be so for real. You know I'm on a diet. I'm not eating all that sugar," I said to her.

"These ain't for you! These is for the man," she yelled.

We busted out laughing because I knew she was dead serious. Aunt Vi left to put some of the cookies in a plastic bag. I saw a sexy nightgown. I packed it discreetly.

The next morning, I dropped my suitcase by the door in the living room and nonchalantly spoke to Ryan. I headed back to my room and stopped dead in my tracks. I turned around. Ryan handed me a manila envelope. I set down my laptop bag and took a look at it.

"Aunt Vi let me in before she left. She said you'd be out soon. I wanted you to have this for your commute. I read it last night, and it's layered. I know it was a last-minute client, but the word *acquisition* is mentioned a little too casual for my taste," he said, full of an unfamiliar concern I rarely saw from him.

"I never regret hiring you. Since you're here, you can drop me off. I'm running late," I told him.

He grabbed my carry-on suitcase, and we left together.

CHAPTER 4

I found a cozy window seat and slipped into the thick leather seats on the train. I did a lap around my phone before deciding to play *The Best of Alicia Myers*. I drifted off to sleep, and when I woke up, I was at Evan's house. It looked just like Lance and Mia's house in *The Best Man Holiday*.

He opened the door for me, looked me up and down, and scooped me up. I wrapped my legs around him, and we kissed like we were in high school. *He held me up by my ass while closing the door with his other hand, not missing a beat. He allowed me to slide down his muscular body until I was sitting on the couch, kissing his stomach.* He sat on the coffee table, meeting me eye to eye.

"I've been following you for years. When one of our friends told me you were single, I knew it was my chance to step to you and do my demonstration. Sydni, you are the most beautiful woman I've ever laid my eyes on. I don't want to waste your time, so I'm putting it all out on the table. I'm ready to have real love in my life, and I plan to spoil you and make your life so easy you never need to look to another person for another thing," he professed.

My heart was beating so loud I could barely hear him over my pulse. I knew God was real, but this was too good to be true. I kissed him to make sure he was real. He tongued me down so good my panties came off by themselves. His touch felt so good. I felt important and small all at the same time. I felt safe from harm—safe enough to let go. And I knew I had just met this man, but he was speaking my language, and I trusted that even if it was only for this moment, we were on the same page. So I allowed myself to have him—all of him.

"Miss, miss. I'm sorry, miss…" A foreign voice grew louder and louder.

I thought it might be Evan, but he was so busy kissing me there was no way he could be talking too. Right?

"Miss, we have arrived in New Jersey. I'm going to have to ask you to depart the train, or you'll be headed back to the city," said an older man looking over me.

I opened my eyes. My hands were in my pants, and the entire train was empty except for me, the old man, and the cleaning team. I grabbed my things and got the hell outta there.

About forty-five minutes later, I was pulling up to a house similar to the one in my dream. I peered out of the window. The mansion was massive, constructed of classic brick with stately white columns framing the large double-door entrance. Warm light glowed from within the windows. I blinked to clear my sight of the storybook charm—but it was real. It was dreamy.

The driver opened my door. I followed him with my luggage as I took in the perfectly crafted shrubbery. The oversized front door opened, and a large, intimidating Black man was standing on the other side.

"You must be Miss Cole," he said.

"I am. Evan?" I pretended. I knew damn well he wasn't Evan, but it was too early in the game to choose sides.

"No, Mr. Sterling had some delays. He'll be here in an hour or so. I'm his chief of staff—sometimes security—Rashad," he said.

I shook his hand and told him it was nice to meet him. Rashad was a calm fine. He kinda put me in the mind of Beyoncé's Julius. He was a quiet terror—the kind of man you wanted to be in trouble with, but you didn't want any trouble with. And even though I could see how there was probably a woman sitting by the phone waiting for his call, he wasn't my type.

One thing I understood about myself was that I was too much of a control freak to be with a man who took orders. I was already overwhelming for most men, but since clawing my way out of Juke's ego, I was exhausted from catering to men who needed me to shrink. I needed a boss who cared nothing about what I did. Something told me that wasn't gonna be Rashad, but I could tell instantly that he was a good man. Maybe for Liza.

Rashad grabbed my luggage. I reached in my purse for cash—really slowly because I didn't actually want to tip the driver.

"Your money's no good here," he said.

I loved when men said that. Rashad tipped the driver handsomely and ushered me inside. Yeah, he was gonna be great for Liza.

Once inside, I took in the home—expansive yet inviting. My mouth hung open, taking in the sweeping staircases, high ceilings, and grand living room. I had to reel it in and act like I had been somewhere, but Rashad was clocking my tea. It was like he expected it.

"You know, I don't usually stay alone in big houses with six-foot Black men, but something tells me I'm safe," I said to him, officially offering him my friendship.

He laughed and let me know he was six-foot-six, and I was indeed safe. I instantly felt like we'd be friends for years. He handed my luggage off to a butler and showed me around the house. Apparently, Evan was running a little later getting in from the city, so this was the perfect opportunity for me to gawk at the house without him seeing drool fall from the corners of my mouth.

Evan had an indoor Olympic-sized saltwater pool and a spa with a staff on hand for manicures and pedicures. He had a chef, a personal driver, and of course, Rashad—security and chief of staff. When Rashad offered me lunch and a massage, I heard my aunt's voice pop in my head telling me, *"Let him do the things he offers to do."*

I said yes to the food, the massage, and the mani/pedi. Rashad laughed at me like a big brother.

"Right away, Miss Cole," he said.

"Please, call me Syd," I replied.

"Syd. We're happy to have you," Rashad corrected himself.

He pointed me in the direction of my suite. My phone started to ring, and I made sure he was occupied with the chef before answering. It was Liza. I answered, and she immediately asked if I was pregnant. I couldn't even lie to her. I never dealt with men who didn't have it, but this was another level. I could absolutely see how a woman could walk in here and roll the dice on unprotected sex.

"He's not here yet, but he arranged for me to have a chef-prepared lunch, manicure, pedicure, and an indoor Olympic swim if I want to," I bragged.

Then she told me it had a grotto. She'd checked out the place on Zillow when she made my travel accommodations. I couldn't even be mad at her. She always had my back—and a little bit of nosiness to go with it.

Liza proceeded to tell me how the house was gonna be mine and that I should just lean back and not lift a finger. She was all the way into our third child together when I had to remind her that I was indeed there to work and this man didn't know me from Jack.

"Syd! You gotta plan for the night you wanna have. Hurry up and get your nails done before the man mistakes you for a kangaroo. Syd, come on! Are your legs shaved? Are your panties cute? Did you floss your back teeth?" she screamed so loud I had to lower the volume on my phone.

Liza was right. I hadn't truly treated this like it was a potential love connection. I had completely neglected my beauty regimen while leaning into my work to get over Juke. But the last thing I was about to do was let Juke get in the way of me getting true love. And I didn't know if Evan was gonna be it, but he was practice at minimum.

"Rashad! I'm ready for my nail appointment!" I yelled.

My hands and feet were perfect as they slid across the sheets on top of the massage table while I got twisted from east to west. Rashad knocked respectfully and then entered to let me know that Evan had arrived and was working in his study whenever I was ready to join him.

I got my back cracked and tiptoed back to my room. I went to get dressed and couldn't figure out if I should be in sweats or business casual. It was such an unusual working situation. And I was so relaxed I felt like I should be slipping into some soft cotton and curling up with a bowl of popcorn.

Wait. I didn't know this man. This was my first time in the house, and sure, Rashad seemed cool—but I didn't know him either.

I put together a relaxed hunter-green blouse and trousers from Veronica Beard, shook my large rollerset curls loose, and brushed my teeth. Liza called back, but I opted out of talking to her. I didn't want her psyching me out or putting more thoughts into my head. Then she called again, and I answered.

She inspected my hands and feet. She wanted to check my bikini line, but I had to draw the line somewhere. She asked if the staff was there all the time or if he just rented them when he occupied the space.

"It's not my business because I'm here to work, and that's not my man," I said, standing firm on my 'professionalism.'

That's when my auntie chimed in on the convo, and I realized that Liza was at my place and not her own.

"I came to bring her some dinner since you abandoned her, and then we started wedding planning. Keep talking nasty, and I'm gonna make Auntie my child's godmother instead of you," Liza threatened playfully.

Auntie enjoyed that. She asked to see Evan because he was cute online.

That prompted me to look for my laptop. I stopped dead in my tracks, knowing something was wrong. I started tearing the room apart. Liza could see me panicking.

"I can't find my laptop. I never leave home without it, let alone travel without it. Oh my God. This is so amateurish. This man is waiting on me right now. Did I leave it in the black car on the—"

Aunt Vi held up a laptop in the camera. I was relieved—briefly. Because if my laptop was there, that meant it wasn't here.

"I'm supposed to be on my way up the stairs to meet this man and present my ideas to save his entire empire, and I do the one thing I never do and leave my laptop at home? How does this even happen?" I whisper-screamed. I was melting down. The walls were closing in fast again. I could hear Evan and Rashad talking outside my room. I went into my personal bathroom, closed the door, and slid down the wall in a dramatic manner.

"What are you, in a music video? Get up. I can run it up there to you. What time is it—five p.m.? I can get on a train and be there before eight," Liza offered.

But it was Christmas Eve Eve. I couldn't let her do that. I considered asking Ryan, but I was sure he was somewhere riding a mechanical bull by now. Then I thought—Rashad for Liza. Actually, yes. I told her I'd make sure to alert security that she was coming.

I hung up and found a notepad in my purse. When I exited my room, I could hear Masego ushering me upstairs. That one song where he was singing lyrics but it didn't have words. I guess the girl's name was Day-Day but I never knew the actual name of the song. I walked toward the sound. The house appeared to be empty. I fussed with my hair as I crept carefully upstairs. I slipped and fell down a couple of steps, making more noise than I cared to admit. I regained my composure, making sure no one saw me. Then I just ran up the stairs.

The music got louder as I approached the study. The double doors were wide open. I saw Rashad leaning up against a desk talking to another man I couldn't see yet. They were discussing delivering presents to children for the holidays—but somehow it sounded so damn sexy. I continued to eavesdrop for a bit just to make sure they didn't say anything crazy about me but quickly bored of their topic. I gave a gentle knock at the door.

A broad leather office chair swung around, revealing a delicious, handsome, fit man—mid-forties—wearing business casual like the end of a shift. There was something cerebral about him. Commanding.

Finally, this was Evan Sterling.

He was something kinda perfect. Sophisticated. I could tell by the Perpetual Calendar Vacheron Constantin timepiece on his wrist, but his beard was full and scruffy. His Brunello Cucinelli chevron button-down was crisp but unbuttoned to his solar plexus. I could see under his desk that he'd paired it with some Levi's, suggesting he did it all for fun. *That told me he'd stroke me while looking deep into my eyes—which was actually everything I needed to know.*

I felt him taking me in. I didn't shy away from the eye contact. We were both a little stunned. Social media and news articles did this man no justice. I was starting to see the shape of our son's face when he snapped me back into the moment.

"Hi, Sydni. I'm Evan. I'm really glad you're here. My apologies for running late—there was a rush getting out of the city. There's supposed to be a storm," he said, extending his hand.

I took it, held on to it, and returned the pleasantries.

And because Rashad was a smart friend with great social cues, he got the hell outta there.

"I'll leave you to it," Rashad said, excusing himself.

That prompted me to inform him that Liza was on her way and that she would need access to the property. Evan offered to send a car to pick up the laptop so Liza could stay clear of the storm, and while that completely made sense, I didn't want to miss the opportunity for her and Rashad to meet. I had to think fast.

"I actually think the train to a car would be faster. I spoke to her about twenty minutes ago. She's already on her way. If that's okay," I said quickly.

Evan backed down, and Rashad promised to make sure it was a seamless exchange. Then he left. And for a moment, Evan and I just looked at each other—not saying anything but somehow saying everything.

CHAPTER 5

A couple of hours later, we were a lot more relaxed and comfortable with each other. Remnants of tapas and small bites from the chef were strewn across his desk, my notepad was full of scribbles, and he was leaned back in his chair so deep you'd think it was a recliner.

"You were part of the problem. You created one of the biggest apps that kept people apart," I said lightheartedly.

"That couldn't be further from the truth. My app was different. That's not what we did. On my app, you could only match with one person at a time," he shot back emphatically.

Unable to sit still, Evan got up and started lifting the hand weights in the corner of the room. I swiveled around in my chair to keep an eye on him. His shirt was now completely unbuttoned. I was waiting for it to come all the way off.

"That didn't make any sense. With all the people you had to filter through, you needed to be dating at least three people at a time to find The One," I replied.

He summoned me over to a set of weights, quietly instructing me to join him, but he never stopped talking.

"And see, I thought that was the problem. We were all looking over our shoulders, thinking that better might be around the corner. That's why I called the app 'Bird in the Hand.' Because that's better than two in the bush," he explained.

I was intrigued. I hadn't personally spent a lot of time on dating apps because I didn't need to, but I'd heard plenty about them. This one sounded intentional and forced its members to be intentional too. I leaned in and began to ask questions—not just because I was working to understand the company so I could learn how to fix it, but also because I might have been one of his next clients.

He went on to explain that users could see profiles and get in each other's queues, but you couldn't see your queue until you broke it off with the person you were matched with. So you were kind of just floating in space, hoping your number got called.

"Some people are worth waiting for. We wanted everyone to have the confidence of knowing that whoever they matched with was single and had taken the time to sit with themselves," he said, like it was all carefully thought out. I still wasn't sold. Who wanted to just be waiting around to get picked? What was this—a middle school flag football team?

He checked in with me before switching to push-ups. He saw my apprehension because I wasn't trying to hide it. I was, however, trying to hide that this man was getting sexier by the minute. His muscles were growing and the sweetness of his sweat was working on me. He was smart and purposeful. He was genuinely kind. Even though I was professionally sparring with him, I felt more relaxed as the night went on.

"It's a really effective process. We have the highest conversion to marriage of any of the apps, and we've only been on the market for four years. It's actually encouraging people to lean in and give love a chance to blossom. Society's microwave now. All these sped-up videos make us think that a five-hour process should be done in sixty seconds. Love takes time," he said, very sure of himself.

By this point, I was holding the weights to humor him. I wasn't working any muscles. So there was no resistance when he lay on his back and summoned me to stand over him so I could throw his legs to the ground, creating the best ab workout ever. This would've been a lot more fun had I worn a skirt.

"Don't you ever think to yourself that you created a hookup app that encouraged people to stay home and scroll rather than go out and meet the love of their lives?" I asked.

He went on to defend his company, suggesting that times had changed and people used social media to date anyway. I couldn't argue with that.

I was starting to realize why he was being sued. His platform promised sacred love. So when one of the members was assaulted on a date, it felt like a failure of terms and conditions. I told him we needed to restore the trust of the online community and re-center love as the focal point, not marriage. He asked how long I'd been with my man. I didn't typically discuss my personal life with clients, but I was in this man's house, eating his food, and had used his nail techs. Plus, it felt like his question could somehow lead back to the work we were doing on his app. So I did something I rarely did—I opened up and let my guard down.

I told him I was recently "ensingled." And while he'd never heard that word before, he knew exactly what it meant.

He asked if my work schedule had anything to do with the breakup. I found that offensive but tried to mask it and play it cool. "His work schedule was demanding, predictable but hectic. I actually went into business for myself so I could be more flexible to support him," I said.

"Yet you chose to work on Christmas Eve," he said nonchalantly.

"You don't know me. You don't know my background. You have no idea what I've been through. I take care of me," I snapped. Cover blown. Evan quickly realized that he had stepped in some muddy waters. I tried to pull it together.

"Let's focus. I understand how your app functions and why the domestic dispute between your subscribers is detrimental. You've said some things I don't disagree with," I tried to press forward.

"You could just tell me I'm right," Evan said. I was so turned off.

"Is that what you need to hear?" I asked, challenging him.

He laughed at how mad I was getting, which pissed me off even more. Like, sir, I was about to give you the chance to pursue me, and here you were morphing into an asshole right before my eyes. I could feel the attraction leaving my body.

"If I'm right, I'm right. Am I right?" he said, feeling himself. "Listen, every time I fall in love, I lose time and money. And I'm no longer willing to compromise those things."

"What happened to 'Love takes time'?" I reminded him of what he said earlier—half looking for him to eat his words, half asking him to restore my faith in him being worth my time.

"It does. Just not mine. I make the rules," he said, sure of himself. Confirming my suspicions of him being an asshole, but also re-establishing my attraction.

"When's your birthday?" I asked.

He rolled his eyes, already anticipating my line of questioning.

"I'm a Taurus, and everything they said about me is true," he replied with unshakable confidence.

"I asked for your birthday," I said, rolling my eyes. "Let me ask my damn question."

"So you can make a snap judgment about my personality based on my zodiac sign? We have a premium feature on the app for people who only want to be visible to those compatible with their signs."

He had clocked my tea—and I was turned on.

"Let me guess... Virgo," Evan teased, knowing he had me against the ropes and refusing to back down. I laughed in admission.

"I looked you up. Virgos pay attention to detail. That's part of the reason I wanted to hire you," he said, carefully disarming me.

"You all can be a little controlling, but that's just how women are. At least with you, it comes with a work ethic to make up for it," Evan said with ease.

"Excuse me?" I yelled, not expecting the knife or the twist.

Evan laughed and shrugged as if to say, "It's not my fault." I was pissed.

"It was a joke," he copped out. But it was too late—my attraction had dried up again. Not only was he an asshole, but a misogynistic asshole.

"Can we just focus on the app?" I said, heading back to the desk. I was over the workout, the conversation, and the powwow.

"This is my company, my house, and my time. I call the shots around here," Evan said, standing to his feet.

I couldn't believe this had taken such a nosedive. I looked at him in disbelief. Arguing with another man I wasn't even sleeping with wasn't on my bingo card.

"Whoa. You got it. I think we're done here," I said and immediately started gathering my things.

Liza peeked her head between the double doors. Her face was so beautiful and full of joy, even though I knew she'd heard at least some of what had transpired. Evan closed the distance between us. Instant regret.

"I'm sorry. I was out of line," he whispered.

Liza feigned concern. "Everything okay in here?" she asked.

I nodded. Liza handed me my laptop, checking in with me for real this time. I told her I was fine and introduced them formally, which took some of the focus off me and Evan. He whisked Liza under his charm, discussing reimbursement for her travel and her plans for the holiday. I almost forgot Christmas was in two days—not that it made much difference.

I was grateful to have my computer, but now that Liza was talking about rushing back to avoid the storm, I was jealous. I wanted to go with her. Back home. Back where it was safe. Evan noticed my unease. Rashad made his way into the office with apprehension all over his face. We all shifted.

"What happened?" Evan asked, prepared to protect us all.

"It's not looking good," Rashad said. "The snow is picking up. We could probably make it to the store before it really hits, if you need anything." I held my breath, thinking about Aunt Vi.

"No, no. We're good here. Send the staff home to their families. It's the holidays," Evan said, looking out the window.

"I'll do that. And Liza, I think it's best if you don't try to get back into the city in this weather," Rashad warned her.

It was really convenient that we were all snowed in together, even though I couldn't detect any romantic undertones yet. Liza had just gotten there. I hadn't even had a chance to see if she was feeling Rashad in a real way. The snow was coming down hard, and the men were making decisions without us even consulting each other.

Evan stepped in. "He's right. We've got everything you might need."

At that point, we had to make a choice. Liza checked in with me. I was still uncomfortable with staying in Evan's house after experiencing his slick mouth. I started researching the weather on my phone. If it wasn't absolutely necessary, I didn't want to stay. We could Zoom from anywhere, and I didn't want Aunt Vi over there all by herself in the storm.

"Hey, I'm not holding you here," he said, slightly offended. "You're free to go. We can finish this on Zoom if you want. You can go now."

I was pissed off all over again. Like, sir, you just apologized for coming at me sideways, and then you wanted to double down? Offending me wasn't enough, so I leaned into making him feel bad.

"My aunt is at home by herself. The holidays are one thing, but a blizzard is another. I don't feel comfortable leaving her to fend for herself," I said tenderly.

Embarrassment washed over Evan. Blizzard wind sounds whipped outside the window. Snow poured down. I deflated, genuinely. Rashad pulled me to the side and met me at eye level to comfort me and remind me of the friendship we'd established before Evan took us off the rails.

"Just tell me what you need. I can make it happen, but I gotta keep you safe," he said.

I told him I just needed to call my aunt and make sure she felt okay. I liked the attention I was getting. I liked Evan not de-escalating the situation. And I liked my concerns being heard.

I went back to my room downstairs. Liza sat on the bed while I paced back and forth, waiting for Auntie to answer the phone. She sounded fine. I could hear the news in the background, synced up with the muted TV in my room. Auntie insisted that she was fine but mentioned it would've been nice to have some water on hand. Liza immediately sprang into action, trying to get water delivered to the house, but all of the courier sites were paused because of the storm. I panicked.

"Girl, calm down. Ain't no sense in you being all the way up there and worried about me. I've weathered many storms, and you weren't even alive for half of them," she joked, reminding me who the real adult was. "As long as you and Liza are together, and y'all got some big strong men looking after you, I won't worry."

I assured her that we were fine and eventually got her off the phone. I paused for a second, still worried. Liza was on the same page.

"Yeah, I don't like it either. You wanna call Juke, don't you? Get him to take some stuff over there?" Liza asked, confirming my thoughts.

She was spot on. I figured if we both had the same idea, it must've been the right one. So, I called Juke's unsaved number on speakerphone but turned the volume down just in case he said anything crazy. Liza and I hovered over the phone. He answered, happy to hear from me.

"Hey, yeah. I'm out of town working with a client, and it looks like I'm getting snowed in out here. Can you go drop some stuff by my place for Aunt Vi? She's all by herself," I asked in the most pitiful voice I could muster.

He was so eager to help, I could hear him getting dressed. Liza had to muffle her laugh. It kinda melted my heart a little—to hear him so invested in my relief that he was willing to personally go out into the snow to take care of my auntie.

When I hung up with him, I felt better. Liza did too. She asked if it made me want to be back with him, but the problem was never Juke caring about me or my auntie—it was him being willing to pledge his devoted love to me and build a future with me. I admitted to feeling relief in that moment, but I knew it was fleeting. Marriage was about feeling it all the time. Liza reminded me of how unrealistic that was. But I didn't care. I knew I deserved more than what he was giving me—but for today, I'd take the groceries and batteries for my auntie.

Now that that was squared away, I could finally get my questions asked.

"Bitch, are you feeling Rashad or what?" I asked with all the enthusiasm I could muster.

She snatched me onto the bed to silence me, and we cackled like schoolgirls.

"Girl! He's the most beautiful man I've ever seen. Did you see him?" she said innocently.

I laughed because my best friend was already in love—just like I'd predicted.

"Syd, I can see myself having his baby. I can tell by how he takes care of us he'd be a really good dad. He picked me up from the train station, and within minutes, we were holding hands," she said, drifting back into her memories. "We didn't even talk about it. He just held my hand, and I held his back. Am I in a fuckin' dream?!"

"He seems like a really good dude. Just don't jump in too fast before you see his real personality," I said, trying not to let my disappointment about Evan show.

"No, Syd. I'm gonna stay right here. What if this is the real him? What if he's this sweet, this kind, this protective? What if it's real and nothing ever worked out with anyone else—not because it wasn't supposed to, but because it was supposed to work out for me and him? What if this is the best thing that ever happened to me?"

Liza asked every question with a deeper level of hope and certainty. I always admired that about her. Even when I was distracted by disenchantment, she always held enough optimism for the both of us. I rested in the comfort of her dreams and laid my head on her shoulder. I believed her.

"This is your husband," I assured her.

She grabbed my cheeks and looked me dead in the eyes.

"And Evan is yours. And he's sure. He's not dragging you on for years. You came into his life and made it better, and he realized he needed to be a better man to be with you. So he spent the rest of his life rising to the occasion," Liza said with such precision that it brought tears to my eyes.

I decided to agree with her. It wouldn't make anything worse to just believe he was my man and this was my house and this was our life for the next couple of days. I'd be no worse off when I left.

"Yeah. We're the girls who get it all," I professed.

"We are the girls who get it ALL," she affirmed.

CHAPTER 6

I decided to take a shower and wash off the day. The oversized tile on the floor made me feel small and precious. I was careful to enjoy the hot water but not let it ruin my hair. Tension left my shoulders as the water pressure massaged my back. I thought about Evan. He was a hothead. A sexy hothead, but a hothead nonetheless.

I wondered if that would weaken over time if he fell in love with me—or increase as I grew to need him. Regardless, I didn't feel safe enough to even like him. Against my own will, I realized I'd need courage to forgive him and continue with anything personal—that's if I hadn't completely gotten on his last nerve.

We'd both have to want to be loved more than we feared falling in love with each other. That thought was scary, especially because I wasn't sure I was done loving Juke.

Wait! That was the answer to rebranding his company: the members of his community would need to find the courage to continue to love, even though it was scary. Even though someone got hurt. Even though love had no guarantees. That was it! I was ready to work.

I had used over a hundred dollars' worth of water on my 5'5" frame that wasn't even close to being dirty. I got out and rubbed body oil into my skin while it was still damp. I'd been taught to do that when I was young to ensure my skin didn't crack during the winter. I slipped into those cozy sweats I'd been eyeing earlier. I'd packed them to travel back in, but now that I was trapped and clothes were limited, I figured I might as well be comfortable.

When I opened my door, I could hear Liza holding court with the guys in the kitchen. I took the opportunity to creep back upstairs where I'd left my computer and get some work done.

I made it back into the office undetected. I sent D'Angelo crooning through the speakers and wired in. I built the new campaign around having the courage to love.

After an hour or so, I was deep in a groove. It was closing in on 10 p.m. by that point. Evan knocked gently on the door and let himself in—it was his house, after all.

"I don't want to disturb you if you're working, but the chef left some food. Thought I'd bring some up as a way to say 'I'm sorry,'" Evan said, setting a colorful plate of food down in front of me.

I checked his face. He looked sincere. I didn't see the point in keeping the line in the sand. I wasn't upset anymore. My auntie was fine. Liza was safe. He'd apologized.

"Thank you. And no, you're not bothering me. I'm glad you're here. I can run some ideas by you," I said, finalizing the truce but keeping it professional.

I walked him through some of my ideas and proposed we do a live event for the members, where they could shake his hand and display their courage to love when it got hard. His eyes lit up. I knew I had him.

He picked me up and spun me around. Then he caught himself. We both retreated.

We spent the next few hours working and fleshing out the idea. By the time Liza and Rashad came up with a tray of my auntie's cookies, I was on top of the desk in the Nicki Minaj challenge and Evan was doing pull-ups.

They were so confused—but it was also extremely funny.

"I promise we're working," I assured her.

Evan laughed it off and tackled the cookies like I was going to fight him over them.

"You do realize those are *my* auntie's cookies," I said.

"Well, why aren't you eating any?" Evan asked with his mouth full.

I grabbed a napkin and wiped some of the chocolate from his beard, which was Rashad's cue to leave. Liza went with him.

"Because this isn't my dessert of choice. Some of us have a more sophisticated palate," I said, as refined as I could manage.

Evan rolled his eyes and teased that I must like Swiss Cake Rolls. I playfully punched him.

Accepting the dare, he pinned my hands behind my back, demonstrating his size and strength. It was exciting. I pressed into him, an open invitation if he was ready to kiss me and make all of my dreams come true. We both sat in the tautness, and then he retreated.

I went back to my seat in front of my computer to get back to work. He went to the other side of the room to throw darts. It got quiet. Eventually, we talked more about the company, the rebrand, our childhoods, and even about what the future owed us.

Before long, it was 3 a.m. Evan was asleep on his chaise, and I was fading fast. I knew I was sleepy, but I had a choice to make: go to my room or lie on top of Evan.

Now, I wasn't sure if the second option was actually an option, but I did know that faith honored boldness. I figured I should overthink it for a minute—would I be satisfied if I went downstairs and went to sleep, or would I be down there thinking about being up here with him where I already was? I decided to test my luck.

I lifted the thin blanket off of Evan and crawled on top of him. He stirred a bit, surprised to be looking into my eyes but comforted by my body. I laid my head on his chest. He cradled me snugly until I synced my breathing with his heartbeat—and before I could stop the drool from leaving my mouth, I drifted off to sleep.

CHAPTER 7

It had to be close to 4 a.m. when I lay on my back, Indian style, balancing a broom between my toes while I spun it in a circle, talking to Juke. We used to call this "kirk mode," where you were so deep in conversation you didn't even realize you'd ended up lying on top of the refrigerator because you were talking to the apple of your eye. I was all of sixteen, and my heart and eyes were wide open.

And baby, two weeks after Homecoming, Juke was that and more. He was seventeen with a donk and a motorcycle. To be clear, a donk was an old school classic car fixed up with candy paint and matching rims. He was his own man, raised by a soft-spirited Black mother and a free-spirited white father. Juke moved like an adult—or maybe his parents just didn't care, because boys don't bring the babies home.

"Let me pick you up from school tomorrow," Juke insisted. He always wanted to pick me up from school. He was in a program that allowed him to leave early to get "on-the-job" experience. Juke didn't always go to work, though.

"I gotta stay after school. You know I'm on the morning news—I have to turn my package in," I protested regretfully. We went to different schools, so I wanted as much time with him as I could get.

"So." Juke was unfazed by my commitment to my work, even as kids.

"So, I don't need a ride if I still gotta be at school. I gotta edit. Avid is on the computer at school."

"Well, let me at least pick you up and take you to Wendy's, get you something to eat, and I'll bring you back," he bargained.

"Why would you come all this way?" I asked. I wanted him to convince me. I wanted him to protest. I wanted him to beg.

"You don't never let me do nothing for you." He ended it all right there. I had no more fight in me. I wanted to see him—and truth be told, I wasn't going to be able to sit still in school all day waiting for that final bell to ring.

So, I let him. He was right. I'd heard he had a job as a lifeguard, which was a really responsible job for a teenager, but I'd also heard he was into other things that weren't so responsible.

He could stay up as long as he wanted. But when I heard the garage door roar, I was reminded that I couldn't. My mother worked nights. We'd been here many times before, so he knew if I hung up abruptly, not to call me back.

As I closed my locker, grabbing the books I needed, I saw Londa. She was wearing some football player's jacket and, to my knowledge, had no idea that Juke and I even knew each other. We never really got along because she thought all the boys belonged to her, but at this moment, we were cordial. It might have started off as revenge, but Juke was charming. He was funny. And he was the ultimate bad boy. Building a connection with someone who didn't attend your high school took real effort. It took… dates. Juke was doing all of that. So, Londa was no longer a factor.

"Hey," Londa said dryly—not with an attitude, just tired from the day.

I spoke back and kept it moving. The timing synced, and we ended up walking next to each other. Our peers passed by, wrapping up conversations. Football players ran toward practice. Nerds carefully carried some contraption. Liza saw me and was confused. Without stopping, I told her I was just going to get something to eat and that I'd meet her in the editing bays. Even in high school, she was there holding me down.

As we exited the school and entered the car pickup area, Londa and I were still walking in tandem—not really talking to each other, more talking with others around each other—but when we landed at the pickup area, we were suddenly the only two Black kids waiting. It got awkward.

She made some small talk to fill the silence. It was better than pretending we didn't see each other.

Then, suddenly, a 1970 Mercury Cougar with blue custom candy paint whipped around the corner, playing *"I'm a Thug"* by Trick Daddy, chopped and screwed.

I watched Londa melt. Maybe a tear formed in her eye. She started walking toward the car. She thought this was the part of the movie where her true love popped up with flowers and candy to surprise her and beg her to come back.

But it wasn't. This was the part of the movie where the girl you couldn't keep up with got into your ex's hot car and rode off into the sunset. *Bitch.*

Classy, Juke leaned over and opened the door for me as the wind whipped my hair and I slid into the front seat. All of a sudden, the entire Black population at school was present to bear witness to the single most scandalous act our high school had ever seen.

Ooo's and ahh's antagonized Londa as Juke made a quick U-turn back down 54th, leaving her steeped in public humiliation. We watched in the rearview until the bass in his speakers rattled her reflection, making her blurry.

Juke and I guffawed like hyenas through the drive-thru. We ordered everything, even though I wasn't hungry at all. I was living off love.

He belted through the teacher's parking lot on three tires, music inappropriately blasting, as he dropped me off at the studio. The timing was perfect because the football team was clamoring to practice, and they feasted on our unlikely coupledom—the straight-A student from the morning news with the football player-slash-suspected drug dealer from the school across the county. He was a celebrated whore, and I was a virgin. We couldn't be more opposite or obsessed.

He kissed me in front of everybody as I got out of his hot car. Pause for reaction from the teenage boys who had been trying to take me down for years.

"I'mma call you tonight," Juke said, solidifying that I was his. He had marked me in front of all the other dogs and affectionately set his ex on fire. I was in toxic teenage heaven.

I got out with my groceries and beamed toward the studio. Liza looked me up and down, shaking her head, then helped herself to my fries.

"You know Londa's gonna try to fight you, right?" she said, munching on the fries I was too happy to eat.

"Do it look like I give a damn?" I shot back.

That's when I felt myself being shaken—but teenage Liza wasn't shaking me. Grown Liza was shaking me.

When I opened my eyes, I was still on top of Evan.

"Me and Rashad made breakfast. We made y'all some plates. Come downstairs," said grown Liza.

Evan and I sat at the massive kitchen island while Rashad and Liza pranced around the kitchen like we had a reservation. The snow was a mile high, and even though the storm had passed, it would take some time for the city to come and clear the roads and make them safe for travel. It was also Christmas Eve by this point, so we could only imagine that the process was going to move slower than it normally would. As I looked around at my friends—new and old—I felt content. I felt grateful. I felt like I belonged.

I had called Aunt Vi, and not only was she safe, but Juke had kept his word and dropped off some water and groceries for her before the storm. That reminded me of Juke. I hadn't even had time to process the dream I'd had about him last night. I didn't even know how close Liza and Rashad had gotten, and every time I tried to be with my own thoughts, these men were in our faces. I wondered if this was what it felt like to be married, because I wanted to be married—but I also loved having my own space.

Evan watched me spin around in my thoughts. "What you thinking about over there?"

"Nothing," I gave my best lie.

Liza noticed I needed to be bailed out and took the reins, captivating everyone's attention. "Okay, around the room. Share one of the most memorable experiences from your childhood. Syd, you're up first."

"Why I gotta go first?" I asked, once relieved and now completely put on the spot.

"Don't overthink it. Like, legit, what's the first thing that comes to mind?" Liza baited me.

Everybody waited in anticipation. And because I didn't have time to be clever and choose something that would somehow make me look good, I told the truth.

The house was upside down. You know that in-between stage where the house gets messier before it gets clean? Yeah, that's where it was. Mama's mania was calming down as we slowly put it back together. Even Daddy was helping.

We were too small to see over the sink, but Mama wasn't letting four hands go to waste. So, my older sister and I stood on crates to do the dishes. We learned how to keep a house early—too early in the eyes of some—but I never met anybody who didn't want to eat my cooking.

Mama told us to go get dressed. Our tiny fingers dripped a trail of water to the bedroom we shared. She was stern, but we knew we weren't in trouble. There was only one occasion that required this level of domestic perfection: Mrs. Valerie was visiting.

I think she was Daddy's coworker at the time, but regardless, Mama looked up to her and wanted to impress her.

The doorbell prompted us to peek through the crack of our bedroom door, our small faces stacked on top of each other to get a glimpse of the only woman who ever made Mama sit up taller.

I knew it was her when I saw her. Mrs. Valerie was fine as hell in her thirties, sporting a *"Not Gon' Cry"* Mary J. golden mushroom cut with one open-faced gold tooth off-center. The perfect blend of ghetto and classy. She hugged Mama and then Daddy. It took her a few moments for her ass to complete its entrance, before her husband, James—tall and handsome—came in behind her. He shook both of my parents' hands before his found the small of Mrs. Valerie's back.

I enjoyed setting the world up for them. Once I had Rashad, Evan, and Liza's trust in my storytelling, I continued and picked up a few years later.

My sister and I were eating a classic burger and fries, pretending not to listen to Mama's conversation with her new friend, Ms. Gina—a train wreck with a good heart. We hated going to Ms. Gina's house because she liked to party, which meant we'd be spending the night since she lived all the way in Tampa, a smooth hour drive from home.

Mama and Daddy had divorced by this point, so we were at Ms. Gina's almost every weekend. One thing I can say about Mama is she had us with her. She wasn't dropping us off. Her cubs were always within earshot, clean, fed, and out of danger.

Then the house phone rang.

"Baby, bring ya auntie the phone," Ms. Gina asked politely. She was always polite—because she was always drunk.

She often tried to force the *"auntie"* title, but I knew exactly who my aunts were. That word wasn't a general term of endearment for an older woman back then. My aunties were in a class of their own, and I refused to disrespect them—but I got up and took it to her.

Into the phone: "Helluh? No, he didn't! No, he didn't! I'm sittin' here with

Jant and the girls. Hold on. We finna come that way!"

Ms. Gina hung up the phone and hopped up like bread in a toaster.

"What happened?" Mama asked, matching her excitement.

"Girlllll, James done bought Val the Lexus!" Ms. Gina beamed.

"No, he didn't," Mama said, already looking for her shoes.

"Yes, he did! Come on! Let's go see it," Ms. Gina squealed. They were practically climbing over each other. You would've thought Shug Avery was coming to town.

Mama rounded us up and we were on our way.

It was a three-minute drive to Ms. Valerie's house, and what I witnessed next was the most pure, genuine, sheer happiness between girlfriends. My sister's and my faces were smashed against the window as we saw them press every button, open all four doors, and blast *"That's the Way Love Goes"* by Janet Jackson. They were in and out of that car like ants—switching seats and gagging at every feature. At one point, James came outside and slow-dragged with Ms. Valerie in the driveway. His hands went straight to her ass. That was the day I knew a man was gonna buy me a Lexus.

Over the years, Mama continued her antics whenever we paid Ms. Valerie a visit. Ms. Val's house was always spotless—baseboards and all. I had been taught to check. Her food was always savory and heavy. Everything had a gravy to match. Her houses got bigger over the years. Her man was always in the other room watching sports. I think that's why Mama looked up to her. Ms. Val was aspirational. Everything had its place. What I wanted Mama to know was that she already had what she was searching for in Mrs. Val. We preferred Mama, her Maxima, and her cooking to any of her friends' any day of the week. But despite our protests, Mama went out of her way to show us the greener grass—even if she couldn't give it to us.

When I finished my story, everybody sat there stunned. I was surprised. I didn't think it was anything remarkable. I honestly hadn't thought much about those times—especially after losing my mom so tragically. I asked them what the big deal was.

"I just never heard you tell that story. I barely even hear you mention your mom anymore. It was so sweet and innocent," Liza said.

"It really was," I admitted. "Her friends weren't always the most sophisticated people, but they all genuinely cared for each other and they were happy for each other."

"That's really beautiful," Evan said, looking at me lovingly. "Kind of reminds me of you two."

We didn't disagree.

"Well, that was just amazing. I had a story in mind, but it was not nearly as wholesome as that," Rashad confessed. We all laughed.

"You're in safe company. It doesn't matter what it is. None of us are perfect," Liza said.

"Fuck it," Rashad said, laughing, and proceeded to recount a story about his dad after his parents split up.

He was visiting his dad. Electricity was moving through his body from the back seat. When the car stopped and turned off, he and his sister raced to the front door. His daddy dragged his feet. They whined at him.

"Alright, alright, alright," his dad said, moving slow, recovering from a full week of work. He unlocked the door and they exploded inside again. Alas. It was Friday night—his favorite night. Blockbuster movie night.

His sister scrambled to get the VHS of *Poetic Justice* from the plastic casing. They were quietly trying to hurry before their dad changed his mind. He and their mama were newly divorced, and when it came to Rated R films, his mama didn't play that.

His dad was the nice one. To me, it sounded like he was trying to win them over. Because time with him wasn't predictable or frequent, they milked it for what it was worth when they got it. Young Rashad went to push the tape in the VCR.

"Aht aht. We had a deal," his dad reminded them. They sighed. Rashad described his dad as a jolly man—a Libra, easygoing, but massive. About six-two. When you're in elementary school, that means your feet swing when you sit on his lap. Young Rashad turned on his small voice.

"Daddy, you said we could watch Janet Jackson," he said. Rashad admitted to having a crush on Janet before he even knew what a crush was. I told him we all did.

"You can. After you watch Michael Jackson. I can't believe y'all ain't seen *The Wiz*, but you've seen *The Wizard of Oz*," his dad said.

I imagined him being something like a hotep—going out of his way to make a big deal about signifiers of Black culture.

"Isn't it basically the same movie?" Rashad's older sister asked.

"Hell naw," his dad protested.

"That movie got lions talking, trees coming alive, and people made outta 'luminum foil. I don't wanna watch none of 'em," Rashad said, unenthusiastic about the mandatory history lesson. But his father put his foot down: *The Wiz first. Then Poetic Justice.*

They slammed their tiny bodies into the couch. They had no idea what they were in for, so they figured they might as well get it over with.

"Y'all want pizza?" his dad asked—the ultimate peace offering. And just like that, he was back on the winning team.

"Yeah, I got a coupon for three large pizzas, any topping, for five dollars," their dad spoke into the phone. He waited. They watched him. Even at eight and ten, they knew that didn't sound right.

"Make the first one pepperoni. The second one meat lovers. And the third, cheese," he went on lying.

"I got the coupon right here in my hand. Three large pizzas, any topping, five dollars," his dad pretended like he was reading it verbatim off a piece of paper.

We were dying laughing by this point because Rashad was full-on acting it out.

He continued, "Dorothy chases Toto's bad ass. The doorbell rings. Finally."

A sheepish white teenage delivery boy stood at the door, bright-faced, holding three large pizzas. His dad tossed him a five-dollar bill with a couple of dollars for a tip and tried to close the door. The kid demanded the coupon, saying his boss told him to ask for it.

Rashad's dad pretended he'd forgotten to hand it over. He invited the kid in politely and launched the most intense search for a nonexistent coupon of all time. With each passing minute, his search grew wilder. He pulled up couch cushions while they sat on them. His anger grew.

"Y'all seen the coupon? Where is it?! I put it right here! I told y'all to stop runnin' around! Get up and help me find it!" his dad yelled.

He was irate. And scary. And lying. They turned the apartment upside down while he shouted so loud the delivery guy finally relented—probably trying to save the kids' lives.

"It's okay, really! I'll take care of it," the delivery guy said, shaking.

"Naw! I got it," Rashad's dad insisted.

"It's cool, man. Really. I got more deliveries. Thanks for your business," the flimsy teenager stammered before scrambling away.

His dad shut the door with a victorious smile, set the pizza buffet in front of them as a silent apology for the yelling, and they accepted—then continued to ease on down the road.

We gave Rashad a standing ovation for his story because—what the hell! It was clear his dad was a character. We all begged to meet him.

"Okay, Liza, you're up," I said, expecting a protest.

"I don't even know what to share. Both of your stories were just so good," she said on cue.

"Nope. We all got stuff. You're in safe company," Rashad teased warmly.

She nodded, picked up what he put down, and started.

"Okay, so the first thing that comes to mind is that weekend when my parents left town," Liza said, glancing at me.

"Freedom Weekend," I screamed, excited.

"Girl, yeah. You remember that?" she asked, as if I could ever forget. "Okay, so we were like fifteen, sixteen? We called it *Freedom Weekend* because we had all the freedom two teenagers could ever want."

We busted out laughing. The guys were enamored by how tickled we were.

I had asked my mom if I could stay at Liza's for the weekend. Spending the night anywhere outside of family was an absolute no-no in my mom's book. She knew the responsibility that came with raising girls and protecting them from predatory men. We were never allowed to spend the night at friends' houses, and it got to the point where I stopped asking. But I'd been friends with Liza for years at that point, and our parents had built a rapport.

Nothing special was happening—but nothing special was happening, so we just wanted to do nothing together. What my mom didn't know was that her parents were leaving town and her college-aged, fine-as-hell brother was driving down from school to "look after us." We kept that detail from my mama.

Her parents had left, and we were waiting for her brother, Johnny, to arrive. Johnny had to be six-one and the color of peanut butter. He'd played football his whole life, so he had the muscles and the abs to prove it. This was the D'Angelo era, so he always kept his straight-backs fresh. I once offered to braid his hair just to get him between my legs. That never happened.

He had a wealth of knowledge about hip-hop and watched *Rap City* like it was a case study. As a preteen, that was all that mattered. I loved talking to him because he rarely gave us the time of day. Liza was vehemently against anyone liking her brother.

I had secretly been daydreaming about Johnny hitting it off with me. Sure, I was five and a half years younger than him, but men liked younger women, right? The boys my age seemed to like me well enough, so Johnny shouldn't be any different. I was sixteen, and I knew I looked mature—grown men flirted with me in gas stations when Mama sent me inside to buy her cigarettes.

But Johnny wasn't like everybody else. He was in college. I figured he was only getting smarter. I'd packed all my weekend clothes that broke dress code at school. I didn't expect anything to happen between us, but it was going to be nice to be in the presence of a real man.

"What you mean he not coming?" I screeched at Liza. I leaned so far into her face, I could smell the meatballs from her Subway sandwich.

Liza hung up the cordless phone with a grin.

"Why are you grinning? Why isn't he coming?" I demanded.

"Girl, chill out. Think about it. Your mama only let you stay because she thought my parents were home. If my brother ain't on the road by now, what's the point? My parents'll be home Sunday morning."

I thought for a second. Johnny had a four-hour drive from his university, and it was already five on Friday. My mama was strict—partly because predators lurked close to home, and partly because my little sixteen-year-old body refused to stay in clothes. But mostly because she didn't want me having *any* fun.

"We got the keys, we got money they left for him that he don't even know about, and we got the whole weekend to ourselves," Liza said, walking me into her vision.

"They left us money?" I asked, eyes widening.

"They left us *money*," she doubled down, fanning out a white envelope made out to "JJ."

"Ain't no way they thought we needed all that for the weekend," I said, stunned.

"This was gas money and a little change for his troubles and gas money to get him back and forth. But since my brother ain't coming…"

"We can't keep their money! Your parents are classy people. That was really nice of them," I said, digging in their cookie jar.

"They got jobs! Plus, if we give it back, they'll know he ain't come. He'd never give it back—and he'll never mention we took it, because he should've never left us here alone," Liza reasoned. She checked to see if I was thinking what she was thinking. I took off running and screaming.

We ran up and down the stairs of the two-story, three-bedroom home like we were in *Home Alone*. Because we were.

The next day, *Mama's Gun* played low as we sat outside some apartments we had no business at. Our bodies spilled out of the tiniest outfits we owned as we checked our reflections in the car mirrors.

"They know we out here?" I asked.

"They should. I told him 1:30," Liza said, scanning upstairs.

"Who is this boy?" I asked, half scared.

"Who, Chin-Chin? He fine, girl. You gonna love him. He got the prettiest curly hair. He always talkin' 'bout how everybody wanna have a baby for him," she said. Chin-Chin was mixed—Jamaican and Chinese—so he was capitalizing on the exotic thing. He was her boyfriend's cousin, so we set up a little double-date situation.

The boys walked out. Jovante, with his dimples and low-cut fade, looked every bit like a football star. Chin-Chin was seventeen, narrow-eyed, with a glorious ponytail of curls and confidence on a thousand.

"Get out, we pushin'," Jovante ordered. We didn't push back.

I was the designated driver since I had my restricts. In our minds, two restricts equaled a full license. Ain't that what they said in *Clueless*?

The car's buttery leather interior glowed under bright dashboard lights—it felt like a spaceship. I pretended I'd been in a Range Rover a thousand times, though I'd only seen them in rap videos. Jovante drove, Liza watched him, and I sat behind her, unbuckled, chatting with Chin-Chin. He lived up to his fine reputation—but lacked personality. I decided to enjoy him for the rumors he'd cause.

We rapped along to Ja Rule and Ashanti and *we had a time.*

"Y'all wanna stop and get food or eat at the movies?" Te asked, bossy as ever.

"I want a big popcorn. It gotta be the big one," I said fast. To this day, it's true—small popcorn makes me feel broke unnecessarily.

"I want some Checkers," Liza said.

"Checkers nasty," Chin-Chin mumbled.

Liza rolled her eyes. "Baby, I want some Checkers," she said, rubbing down Jovante's arm. Next thing we knew, we were in the drive-thru.

We ordered more than we could carry and stuffed it all into a backpack to sneak into the movie.

Once there, me and Liza sat all the way in the back while the previews played.

"You ain't tell me the boy had a Range Rover," I whispered.

"That's his uncle's truck. He let him hold it for away games. He play for the NFL," Liza said, matter-of-fact.

"Te going to the NFL?" I asked, entertained.

"I hope so. He said if he do, he gone get them furs and high-heel Timbaland boots like J.Lo," she said, dreamy. "And I can tell Chin-Chin like you better than his baby mama. Y'all look good together."

"When did he get a baby mama?" I was thrown.

"Girl, hush. It's just a movie. And she still pregnant, and he want a paternity test—so technically there's no child to speak of," Liza whispered quickly.

When the boys came back, she and Te devoured each other while the couple on screen argued about tacos.

After the movie, we ran into kids from school in the lobby. Liza bragged about the Range Rover like it was hers. It was chaotic and loud and beautiful. All the kids our age was headed to see the same movie we had just seen. We ended up seeing the movie again just for fun, then grabbed more food and went to Te's house. His mama was home but stayed in her room. We figured sleeping in a house with an adult was safer than an empty one.

Te went to his room with Liza, leaving me and Chin-Chin in his little sister's room. She was asleep on the couch, so we took advantage of the privacy.

"Did y'all hunch that night? I can't remember," Liza asked me in real time.

"Girl, don't be putting my teenage business out there like that!" I scoffed.

"Whatever, girl," she said, laughing.

I made out with Chin-Chin, but I didn't sleep with him. The thought of getting pregnant by somebody who already had a baby on the way was crazy. I had never had sex, and I didn't like him like that. So it was a no for me.

"Y'all some fast asses," Rashad joked. Maybe we were—but the whole weekend was pretty harmless.

We stayed with the guys, then eased our way back to Liza's house the next morning. Johnny never came, and her parents never knew the difference.

"Evan, you're up," Liza said, moving things along. "And don't act like you got nothing to share—you've had the most time to think."

Prompted by Liza's movie story, Evan told a story about sneaking into the movies with his brothers.

It started with his mama—lean, honey-skinned, with a '90s French roll to perfection. She poked her head into the bedroom doorway.

"Put on ya shoes. We finna go," she said.

Evan, the oldest, asked, "Where we going?"

"Don't worry 'bout it. Just ride," she said.

He was about eleven or twelve. They rushed to put their sneakers on, knowing Mama had something up her sleeve they'd like.

Later, they got out of the car at the movie theatre. Evan got excited—they rarely went. Blockbuster nights were cheaper.

"What we watching?" he asked.

"Y'all watching *All Dogs Go to Heaven 2*. Me and your daddy watching *A Thin Line Between Love and Hate*. He meeting us inside."

Evan was livid. They didn't watch cartoons at home. He grabbed his little brother's arm, silently warning him not to talk back.

Mama dropped them off with popcorn and disappeared into the dark. Evan barely let the opening credits roll before he pulled his brothers toward the theatre showing *A Thin Line*.

They sat close to the exit—ready to duck out if caught. The baby brother wanted the cartoon, but they couldn't risk leaving him unattended. He couldn't be trusted.

On screen, Martin did that silly walk he does—and a man entered late. Dylan's laugh gave them away. The man turned. It was their father.

He couldn't see into the dark. The other moviegoers were frustrated with him blocking the screen and being tardy so Evan's dad hurried to his seat without confirming his suspicions. Evan pinched Dylan, glaring.

All in all, it was worth it. The little one fell asleep, and they finally relaxed into the film. They almost forgot to leave before the credits rolled.

"We had the time of our lives in that theatre," Evan said proudly. "My brother called me just last week, saying how cool I was for coming up with that plan. It's still one of our favorite movies to this day."

CHAPTER 8

We were all satisfied with storytime, and the men decided they'd take a stab at clearing some of the snow from the driveway before it picked back up later. That finally left me alone with Liza so I could ask my questions.

As soon as the oversized front door slammed shut, I said, "So, how was it?"

Then I paused and remembered.

"I can't believe you asked me if I slept with another man in front of him," I yelped.

"Girl, relax. We were teenagers," she defended herself.

"No man wants to hear about you being with another man. They don't care how long it's been," I said.

"You're right. That's on me. I just didn't wanna forget to ask again. I been waiting to ask you that for more than 20 years," she joked.

"How was it?" I calmed down so I could get what I wanted.

Liza looked me in the eye, grabbed the dishes, and turned her back to put them in the sink. I walked up beside her and folded my arms.

"It was *so good!* Whew! Girl, he was so big and strong and just handled me," Liza gushed. "I was on the fence about whether I was really gonna let this man take me down on the first day we met, but I was like, it's Christmas! *Merry Fucking Christmas!* And baby, it was a present! Girl, it was like —a performance. We just flowed. *He scooped me up like ice cream and stroked me in the air like they do online. I ain't never had nobody scoop me like that.* It was divine. Rashad don't owe me shit. I wouldn't care if it never stopped snowing."

Liza did a pirouette across the kitchen floor. We gagged and ice-skated in our socks to the magic. I was happy for my friend. She did it. She brought it into reality. We celebrated that sex as if he'd bought her a Lexus.

"What about y'all?" she asked, hoping I had a similar story.

"So, no — I actually worked. He fell asleep, and when I couldn't keep my eyes open, I just decided to lie on top of him," I said.

"What?! I can't believe you initiated it. You love to make 'em beg for your panties," Liza said, rolling her eyes.

"Yes, I do like to be cherished," I admitted bashfully. "But I made an exception. It felt safe enough to do. I figured I didn't wanna be in that big-ass bed all by myself. Big-ass bed? Big-ass man? I chose the man."

"I know that's right," Liza replied.

"The part that got me was that I dreamed about Juke all night," I said.

Liza was displeased—ready to throw the whole conversation away. I told her about the dream, which didn't take long, because it actually really happened and she had been there when it did.

"Have you ever dreamt about something that actually happened?" I asked.

"Not like that. Listen, you were with Juke a long time. Of course he's still sizzling around in your subconscious. And truthfully, I'd rather he stay there than in reality," Liza said. "Is dreaming about Juke affecting how you feel about Evan?" she asked cautiously.

"I like Evan. I just don't know if it's gonna work. He's handsome. He's funny. A little on the misogynistic side—but nobody's perfect," I admitted.

"I'd bet on him before I spend another useless year with Juke," Liza said coldly.

I knew she was right, and I knew that comment came from a loving place. It just wasn't so easy to walk away from somebody you'd spent so much time with. I didn't tell her I was secretly wishing Juke would come back and sweep me off my feet. But it had been months, and the most effort Juke had put in was changing his number to send a few texts. To be honest, I'd expected more when I broke it off with him.

"After five years. In your thirties! That should be illegal. I can't wait to see him sick over a new man treating you like farm eggs," Liza continued without my consent. "Syd, listen to me. I think this is your man, girl. Don't ruin it by playing tough and guarding yourself. It's Christmas, and you're here. *Be here*," she said.

Before I could respond, we heard a buzz on the security system intercom.

"Hey Evan! 'Sup, man. It's Juke," the familiar voice said through the speaker.

I couldn't believe what I was hearing. Juke was at Evan's house. I was convinced I was dreaming again. Liza pinched me.

"Bitch, you are *not* dreaming. Juke is outside," Liza whispered.

"But why?! What are we supposed to do? Aren't Evan and Rashad outside? Can he see us? Why is he here — of all places?! Oh my God," I panicked.

Liza ran to the back window and saw Evan and Rashad making their way back to the front of the house with shovels.

"We're about to see. They're headed back to the front," Liza said, grabbing me and dragging me toward a front window where we could see without being seen.

"Shit. They know each other?! What are the odds," I whispered.

"Juke ain't running nothing over here. He's a jerk. I don't care if they do know each other. When it all comes out in the wash, you leaving with Evan. Ain't nobody got time to be accommodating Juke — of all people," Liza whispered back.

The men kept talking. Their body language looked casual, even friendly.

"I can't tell what they're saying," I nudged Liza. We were ear-hustling so hard but could barely hear anything beneath their laughter. "If Juke comes in here, I'm cooked. Liza! What if he comes inside?! He'll make a scene so bad Evan won't even want to be with me anymore. I can't look," I whisper-yelled.

Liza kept looking. "He's coming inside."

We hid behind the elaborate drapes framing the windows just as the door opened. The rooms were so massive they didn't notice us. They walked past the kitchen, and Rashad was the only one actually looking for us.

"Aye, what happened to the shorties?" Rashad asked, noticing the clean kitchen.

"Oh snap, y'all got company? Man, I ain't know that. Y'all in here snowed in and boo'd up. Let me get out y'all way, man. I ain't mean to be all in here cock-blocking," Juke said, genuinely trying to be considerate.

"See? He always puts ass first," I whispered to Liza. She nudged me silent.

"Let me get the updated contract for you, then," Evan said, running up the stairs to his office, leaving Juke and Rashad to chat.

"I ain't know you was married, man. Congratulations," Juke said.

"Oh, I'm not—but this one is special. Yeah, man, I come across a lot of women who just want a purse, but this one? She's sweet. Pretty. Her cooking go crazy," Rashad gushed. "I don't know, man. I ain't saying I'm checking out, but I'm definitely in the basket."

"Oh, you *in* the basket," Juke said, dapping him up.

"What about you, man," Rashad turned it around on Juke.

"Mannnnnn. I'm just taking it easy. Nothing heavy," Juke said casually. "I was with my old lady for a long time but it got to be too much pressure. I'd rather just let her go find what she looking for. Started to feel like I was in the way of some big plan she had."

"She wanted that ring," Rashad said laughing.

"Yeah, man," Juke admitted.

"They all do. Mainly so they can impress each other or stop looking over their shoulder but you know what? So I do, man. When I find her, she ain't gotta ask. I'm sicka these broads," Rashad said playfully.

"These hoes ain't loyal," Juke dapped him up.

"They not. Until one is," Rashad said silencing the laughter and leaving a lot on Juke's mind.

It was actually nice to see men be so vulnerable and expressive about something other than sports. I slowly turned my head toward Liza, and a tear was falling down her cheek.

Evan returned with a manila envelope. He handed it to Juke. "I appreciate you for stopping by, man. It's always good to chop it up witcha," Evan said, escorting Juke outside.

All three of them were back on the front porch, and we were back peeking through the window like kids on Christmas Eve.

"I wanna know how he even got up here. I thought the roads were blocked," Liza said.

"He owns a house up here. He thought I didn't know, but I know everything. I thought he bought it to surprise me, but he's had it for a year and never even mentioned it," I confessed.

I rarely kept things from her, and I honestly planned to tell her I knew when he presented the house to me—but that day never came. I loved that my friend was willing to carry the disappointment with me, but right now we had bigger fish to fry.

"The most important thing is that your man knows you're the one," I said, pulling Liza back into reality.

"Syd, I knew it. I felt it—but I thought it would be at least three months before he felt it. They're always behind us with their emotions. But it's real. It's really happening," Liza said in disbelief.

"It's happening for you," I said, matching her energy.

"For *us*," Liza corrected, looking me dead in the eye.

"It's happening for us," I said, honoring her request.

Out of the corner of my eye, I saw Evan reach for the door, and we rushed back into the kitchen. The guys met us there.

"Where y'all been?" Rashad asked. "We been looking for y'all."

We told them we'd gone looking for them too. The topic shifted quickly, and even though I was grateful this little ordeal let us see Rashad's growing heart for Liza, it still didn't explain what the hell Juke was doing at this house.

Should I just flat-out ask Evan how they knew each other? If I did, it would spark other questions from him. It might make him run—Juke was his homeboy, and he might find me *undateable* after that, which was not what I wanted. What was in that envelope? How well did they really know each other?

It was clear the connection was between Evan and Juke, not Juke and Rashad. Would Liza be able to get the info out of Rashad without sparking suspicion? I'd have to approach this carefully, because the last thing I wanted was to open the door for Evan to start questioning me. Either way, Evan was more valuable to me than Juke. I wasn't about to jeopardize Evan for Juke.

So I'd keep my head on a swivel until I found a way in—but at least I'd know what to look out for.

"You got more groceries in here than Whole Foods," Liza said, rummaging through the food on the counter. "Were you actually gonna cook yourself, Evan?"

"Oh, no. The chef brought those before she had to take off for the storm. If you wanna make anything, help yourself. They're clearing the roads, but I don't know if restaurants will be open later. Our neighbor walked over to check on us. He said he couldn't get his car out of the driveway," Evan said.

"If you cook, it might be nice to invite him over," Rashad suggested.

"No! Umm, not to sound crass, but I think we have the perfect blend of company right here. He's a man. He can figure out how to eat—or starve," I said.

"Sydni," Liza laughed, texting on her phone.

"I think we can put something together. But I did notice you have all the right ingredients for my sweet potato biscuits," I offered, trying to get the men's minds off Juke.

And it worked. Rashad immediately had hearts in his eyes when he heard *sweet potato biscuits*. His mouth watered right in front of us as he asked if I knew how to make the cream cheese frosting and everything. Evan was the only one who hadn't had them. He looked doubtful.

"You don't understand," Rashad raved. "These things so good I almost ate my finger last time I had 'em."

"Y'all mean to tell me everybody around here's been eating sweet potato biscuits for Christmas as a new Black tradition, and nobody told me?" Evan teased.

We tried to warn him, but he kept going.

"Okay, okay, so when we were teenagers, me and Liza came up with our own traditions. We ate sweet potato biscuits and watched *The Preacher's Wife* while we ate them," I said.

Liza's eyes lit up. "Oooo, we haven't watched *The Preacher's Wife* this year!"

"*The Preacher's Wife?* That's not even a Christmas movie," Evan said.

We all said it was—including Rashad. I told them to go see where it was streaming while we made the biscuits. Evan and I locked eyes before he left the room. I could tell he was happy to have a woman cooking in his kitchen because she wanted to, not because he was paying her.

Liza waited for the guys to clear out, then pulled me in close. "Why haven't you read the contract" she asked sternly.

"What contract?" I whispered.

"The reason we're here, Sydni. You were supposed to read your contract before you even packed. Ryan personally brought it over to your house…" she said.

"Making me leave my laptop," I said remembering.

"You don't understand. I've been texting Ryan and he insisted that you read it—and you didn't. So, I would like to say that whatever comes out of my mouth next is not Ryan's fault. Brace yourself," Liza said firmly. "Juke is an investor in Evan's app. Juke was the referral, by way of other people—but Juke is *why* we're here. He doesn't know you're here, but he invested in Evan's company, and when it started to suffer, Juke recommended you," she said, holding for my reaction.

"That's either extremely sweet or…" I said.

"He's trying to control you," Liza finished my sentence. "Don't play in my face, Syd. Read your contract."

She was right. I let her handle the biscuits while I slipped upstairs to get my laptop. I brought it back down to the kitchen so I could at least make the frosting while I read.

When I opened the contract, I couldn't believe my eyes.

Juke, while he had been one of Evan's investors for years, had specifically structured this deal to leverage ownership in *my* company. The contract included one of Juke's subsidiary companies under a different name—which was why it hadn't been an immediate red flag. He was intentionally trying to be part of my success, likely to use it later to leverage ownership or influence—because I broke up with him.

I looked at Liza, tears welling in my eyes.

"I told you," she said softly.

"I hate him," I whispered. "I can't believe he would go this far. What the hell did I ever do to him?" I said, unraveling.

"I know. Just don't fall apart. If you fall apart and blow it with Evan, Juke wins," Liza said.

"Blow it with Evan? How do we know he's not in on it?" I asked.

She hadn't considered that. Honestly, neither had I.

"Okay, you're right. Evan *could* be in on it. But you know what? Love conquers all. He could've come into this with one mind and fallen for you— or maybe he's just a pawn and doesn't know anything. None of that matters right now. What matters is you deciding how you feel about him," Liza said.

"Yeah, and how do I do that?" I asked.

"We're already here. Spend time with him. He invited you. Treat him like he's already your fairytale. Remember—what you see in your reality is only what's being reflected from inside you. If you love you and you want better for you, he will love you and want better for you. You set the tone," Liza said, putting her foot down. "Do the horse test thing with him."

She told me not to mention Juke or the contract. Sign it or don't sign it—but try not to bring it up until I was ready for the answers that came with it. Then she slid the biscuits into the oven and walked away like a mic drop.

I knew this was going to be hard for me. I was used to being in control—and the questions I had about that contract controlled whether I even wanted to be there or not.

CHAPTER 9

An empty plate of orange crumbs sat on the coffee table. Evan reclined on the couch watching *The Preacher's Wife*. I lay on top of him, curled into the nook between his chin and clavicle, trying to be in the moment. I was happy to be watching one of my favorite films with him. He was easy to be around. It hadn't even been twenty-four hours, but I felt something I hadn't felt with a man in years—*secure*.

Denzel started doing that ridiculous 'Popeye' dance just as Evan reached for another sweet potato biscuit. But they were all gone. Keeping his eyes on the TV, he tapped his fingertips against the crumb-filled plate, silently begging for more.

"I guess you hated the sweet potato biscuits," I said, laughing.

"They were so bad, I lost my appetite," Evan replied, tickling me.

I squealed and managed to escape his grip, running across the living room to safety. He threw up his hands in surrender, and I crept softly back to the couch to join him.

The fire crackled like it had something to say. The room was soaked in amber light—the kind that makes you want to tell the truth. Denzel and Whitney were looking more like a couple now—a little jazzy, a little flirty. Enough to make you root for them being together even when you knew it was wrong.

The wine glasses on the table still wore faint stains of red. My laptop was half-open, forgotten. I wrapped myself in a furry blanket that felt too luxurious to belong to me.

Evan sat across from me, watching the flames. I asked if he was going to put up a Christmas tree.

"Nah," he said, shaking his head. "My mother bought a Christmas tree the year I bought this house, and I never put it up."

"Not even once?" I raised an eyebrow.

"Man, that tree's been in there longer than some of the furniture."

I laughed. "That's crazy."

"It is," he said quietly. "I regret it sometimes. It would've meant a lot to her—to uphold the tradition. I just never believed in it." He hesitated, and I could feel the weight before he said it. "We lost her a couple years back."

My heart softened immediately. "I'm sorry," I said. "My mom passed the month before I graduated high school."

He looked at me, his voice gentle. "I'm sorry."

"She had cancer," I told him. My throat tightened, but the words came anyway. "I used to pray so hard that she'd just hold on until graduation. But she didn't."

"That's hard," he murmured.

"That's all I wanted," I whispered. "And when it didn't happen… it kinda made it hard for me to want things anymore. Like—you can pray so hard, and want something real bad, and still not get it. That's crazy."

He nodded slowly. "I been there. So now I just focus on what I can—"

"Control," I finished for him.

"Control," he echoed.

We locked eyes then, and something shifted. We weren't just talking anymore—we were *seeing* each other. Really seeing each other. The space between us felt different.

"I get so jealous when I see people with their moms," I admitted. "I feel cheated. Like there was something in life I might not achieve because everybody else had their mama helping them and I didn't."

He nodded. "I understand that. And I know I've only known you for a short time, Syd, but something tells me there's nothing you can't do. You're the kind of person who can figure anything out. You give other people confidence. You make other people more sure about working for you than themselves.”

I was blown away.

“Nothing is ever going to replace your mom, but you got everything you need to make it,” he said pulling me in for a hug. I needed it. It was like he erased five years of Juke telling me to quit in one statement.

“Thank you for that. I don’t care for Christmas either,” I said. “My auntie lives with me. She put a tree up before I left. I haven’t put one up in I don’t know how long.”

“She didn’t even run it by you?” he asked.

I smiled, a little embarrassed. “I gotta admit, it was beautiful.”

He shrugged. “It’s unnecessary work—putting it up and then taking it down.”

“True,” I said. “But I don’t know. It really was gorgeous.”

He shook his head. “I’m not putting it up.”

“I hear you, but it’s only Christmas once a year,” I said, draining the last of my glass.

When I stood, he gave me a look. “What are you doing?”

“We,” I said, emphasizing the word, *“Are gonna put up the tree.”*

He didn’t move.

“Please?” I added softly.

He sighed. “We?”

“Yes, *we*. Your mama is somewhere smiling down right now, hoping we put that tree up. Now get up and show me where it is.”

I held out my hand. For a moment, he just looked at it—like taking it would mean more than he was ready to admit. Then he reached out and let me pull him off the couch.

"Your nails are really nice," he said suddenly.

I blushed like a little girl, caught off guard.

And then everything turned into a blur of laughter and music.

I couldn't tell you where Rashad and Liza were, but Evan and I dragged the giant cardboard box into the living room, laughing every time we bumped into a wall. I poured more red wine—the bottle nearly gone—and suddenly everything that was funny got funnier. I relaxed more, and Evan somehow got even more handsome, more accommodating.

He handed me ornaments one by one—heavy glass ones, gold ones shaped like stars, little wooden reindeer that must've been his mother's. We wrapped the garland together, our hands brushing as we circled the tree. When I ducked under his arm, I could feel the warmth of him—this big, quiet man who filled every corner of the room without even trying.

Finally, he lifted me—effortlessly, like I weighed nothing—so I could place the star at the top.

From up there, I could see everything: the lights reflecting off his eyes, the soft glow of the fire behind us, and the faintest smile playing on his lips.

For the first time in a long time, Christmas didn't hurt. It felt like something worth believing in again. I tried to savor it as long as I could. It felt so good, so warm, that I wished I could bottle it up and sell it. No—*give* it away. Because everybody deserved to feel like this on Christmas.

We went back to the couch. The streaming service had rolled itself into another Christmas movie. I let Evan sit first so I could decide how I wanted to sit on top of him.

"Can I do this personality test on you that Liza did on me?" I asked, trying to sound innocent.

"I'm showing you my personality now," he said, pulling me back against his chest.

I squirmed away like a cat and sat upright on his lap. "It'll be fun," I insisted.

He took a swig of his wine and obliged. I sat up straighter, excited.

"There's a room. Imagine a room—any room. It just needs to be empty," I began.

Evan closed his eyes and played along.

"There's a box in the room. You see it?" I asked.

He nodded.

"There are flowers in the room," I continued.

"Like, real flowers?"

"Whatever kind you like," I assured him. He nodded again, keeping his eyes closed like a kid. "Oh wait—I forgot. There's a ladder."

"A ladder?" he asked, laughing.

"Yes. It can be wherever you want it. Any of this can be. You just need to see it in your mind."

"What in the Ms. Cleo?" Evan teased, grinning.

"No, really. It's good. Stay with me," I said, suppressing my own laugh.

"I got my ladder," he said. "How much more of this?"

"Okay, there's a horse."

He snorted. "A horse? In my room?"

"You tell me," I said, mimicking Liza's tone.

"I see my horse," he said with mock seriousness.

"Last thing—there's a storm. Let me know when you see your storm."

Evan laughed and finished his glass of wine. "I see my storm."

"Cool! You did great. You wanna know what it all means?" I asked.

"Please. Can I get you some wine first?" he said, tapping my leg to get up.

"Oh, sure," I said, following him into the kitchen.

I sat on the massive stone island, swinging my feet while he opened a new bottle of cabernet sauvignon and refilled our glasses. I took him in—strong, sure, handsome, astute. An intentional man like him deserved an amazing woman like me. It was time to see what was going on in his subconscious.

"Okay, so tell me about your box. Small, medium, or large?"

"Large," he said.

"Of course." I smirked. "Can you see through it, or is it solid?"

"It's solid. What does that mean?" he asked, intrigued.

"So, the box represents you—your ego. The box is big, so there's that. Where was it in the room?"

"The middle," he said.

"Yeah, so you're the center of your world. It's fine. My box was in the center too. Most people are the center of their own world."

"And it being solid?" he asked.

"Oh, that means you're guarded. If it was transparent, that would mean you're an open book. But you're not exactly open or transparent with me," I said, poking the bear.

Evan laughed. "That's not accurate. When's the last time *you* opened up to someone?"

I looked him dead in the eyes. "I'm open now."

"You're not," he said simply. "You're working. You're being *cool* because you're with a client."

I silently admitted he was right. I took a breath. "Okay. I'm open."

I held out my hand to shake on it. He took it.

"Tell me about your ladder," I said, sipping my wine.

He leaned against the counter behind him, one arm flexed to perfection. "It's over by the door. It goes all the way up to the ceiling."

I laughed.

"What's funny?" he asked.

"The ladder represents your drive and ambition. The taller it is, the more driven you are. And yours goes all the way to the ceiling. What's it made of?"

"Steel."

"That means it's sturdy. Nothing's gonna stop you."

"Accurate," he said, smiling. "I like this test. What about the flowers?"

"Right. Where were yours?"

"Sitting on top of the box."

"What kind? How many?"

He tilted his head, thinking. "I don't know the names of flowers, but they were colorful. There were a lot of them—big bouquet."

I smiled despite myself. "Aww. Flowers represent your loved ones, or how many kids you want. And you want your loved ones around you all the time."

He grinned. "Some redemption!"

"Oh, whatever." I laughed. "Okay, your storm. Where was it? How'd you feel about it?"

"It was bad," he said, calm, like he was talking about rain on a Tuesday. "It happens. It'll stop."

"Good." I nodded, studying his face. "Storms represent how you respond to adversity. You see it, you know it'll pass, and you're unfazed."

He flexed his muscles like a joke, and I rolled my eyes. "Okayyyyy," I said, laughing. "Tell me about your horse."

His voice softened. "It was outside, but when the storm happened, I brought it in. It was tied to my ladder."

And something inside me cracked.

I felt my eyes sting before I even realized it. My throat went tight. I couldn't believe it—the tenderness in this man, hidden behind all that muscle and quiet stoicism. I was falling, and it terrified me.

"What now?" he asked gently. "Did I accidentally kill somebody?"

I shook my head. "Not at all. Your horse is your person. And not only did you protect yours, but she's tied to your ladder—meaning your work ethic is directly tied to protecting your person." My voice caught. "That's really poetic."

"It's true," he said simply. "I've been working hard my whole life to provide for my wife and kids. I always wanted to make sure they had everything they could ever want or need. That's why I got this house."

"Well," I said softly, glancing around the wide, echoing home. "You certainly have enough space. Where are they?"

He didn't answer—not with words, anyway.

He leaned across the island before I could think to move, his shadow swallowing mine. His lips found mine, and the world just... stopped. He was so big, so indisputable, and before I knew it, he had me pulled against him, lifted across the counter. I didn't even think—I just responded. My legs wrapped around his waist, my fingers tangled in his hair, and for the first time in a long time, I didn't care what made sense.

"You're my client," I managed between breaths.

He kissed me again. "You're doing an amazing job."

"I don't know about this, Evan," I whispered—half protest, half plea.

He looked at me, eyes steady, grounding. "What is there to know? How do you feel?"

"Good," I said before I could stop myself. "So damn good."

"I want to make sure you always feel good with me," he said.

The room started spinning. And then, just as easily as he had lifted me up, he helped me down from the counter—his hands gentle, certain. He didn't let go. He held both my hands, guiding me out of the kitchen, leading me somewhere I couldn't name.

CHAPTER 10

When I woke up, it took me a second to realize where I was. The sheets were too soft, the air too still, and the arm wrapped around my waist—too heavy to be my own.

Evan.

I blinked against the morning light spilling through the curtains. We were tangled up in his bed, in matching pajamas. I stared down at them, at the ridiculous red plaid pattern that somehow looked good on him and ridiculous on me, and I couldn't help it—this tiny burst of joy escaped me. A private little celebration. *I'm in matching pajamas on Christmas Day!!!*

His room was massive and masculine—lots of woods and deep earth tones. The walls were painted a matte black, making everything look chicer. Before I could process any of it, his arm slid from my waist to my neck, tickling me just enough to spark a pillow fight, which I won, but only because he let me.

"That's how you thank me for making sure you got a good night's rest?" he teased, smirking.

I swung a pillow at him. "You tried to slaughter me!"

He laughed. "Slaughter is extreme. You think you can get some breakfast going? Are you a cooking woman?"

I stopped mid-swing, narrowing my eyes. "You was doing good."

He raised his hands, sheepish. "I asked! I was just asking. I'm sorry, I'm trying. Okay, what should I say?"

"You shouldn't assume that cooking is a gender role," I told him. "Everybody cooks because everybody eats."

He shrugged. "I order. But it's Christmas."

I softened. "What do you usually do on Christmas?"

"Make a sandwich?"

I burst out laughing. "We are not eating sandwiches."

He watched me, a smile tugging at the corner of his mouth.

"Do Liza and Rashad know?" I asked.

He sat up suddenly, motioning for me to do the same. "Wait, sit up."

I followed his lead, tugging the blanket around me.

"Okay," he said. "Now we not pillow talking—"

That sent me over the edge. I couldn't stop laughing.

"What??" he said defensively. "First off, there's nothing to know, because we slept together but we didn't *sleep* together. You were drunk and after you threw up on me, anything freaky was a hard pass.."

My head jerked up. "I threw up on you?"

He grinned. "You threw up on a lot of things, which is why you're wearing different clothes. And, you snore. It's a cute snore. But let's just say Liza and Rashad had their own slumber party. They ain't thinking about us."

"Oooooo!" I teased, wiggling my eyebrows.

As if on cue, Liza's voice echoed from downstairs.

"Syyyyyyyyd!!! Get up! It's Christmas morning! Come downstairs!"

Evan chuckled. "Okay, so maybe she *is* thinking about us."

He leaned in and kissed me.

The family room smelled like cinnamon and coffee when I walked in. Liza was perched on Rashad's lap, sipping cocoa, the two of them framed by the twinkling lights of the tree we had decorated the night before.

"…That's all I'm saying," Liza declared. "If you not posting matching pajamas for Christmas, do you even go together?"

"Right, right," Rashad echoed, pretending to agree while trying not to laugh.

Then they both looked up—and saw Evan and me. In our matching pajamas.

They lost it.

"What?" Evan and I said at the same time.

"Merry Christmas, y'all?" I blurted, desperate to change the subject.

Rashad grinned. "It's thick out there, but last night wasn't as bad as the night before."

Liza opened the window, and a wall of white snow greeted us.

Evan nodded toward the tree. "Don't y'all see the presents under there?"

"Oh!" Liza exclaimed. "That stuff wrapped in paper towels is for us?"

I noticed the small, unevenly wrapped bundles under the tree—makeshift gifts that looked more heartfelt than polished. My chest tightened.

"You did all this while we were sleeping?" I asked softly. "That's just so sweet."

Evan beamed.

Liza grabbed the first gift.

"That's actually for Syd," he said.

She handed it to me and picked up another.

"This one's for Rashad," Evan added.

"Well, is there anything for me?" Liza teased.

"Watch it, Scrooge," I said. "It's Christmas."

"Yeah," Evan said. "That last one is for you."

Liza ripped open her gift—a sleek red box.

"Baccarat Château Baccarat Red Wine Glasses??!?!?" she gasped.

"It's a regift," Evan admitted, laughing. "But I know you like red wine. So I figured they'd get more use at your place."

"That's really cool, Liza," I added, winking. "For your *dinner parties*."

She beamed. "Wow, Evan. Thank you."

"Merry Christmas," he said.

Rashad opened his next—a Rolex, heavy and shining. He turned it over, reading the engraving aloud: *Thank you for watching my time.*

Evan smirked. "What time is it?"

Rashad looked stunned.

"You hold me down all year," Evan said. "And I'm always asking you what time it is anyway. At least now, you got all the time zones on one wrist."

Rashad laughed, shaking his head. "I appreciate that, man. Merry Christmas." They hugged, all warmth and quiet respect.

"Open the box, girl," Liza said to me. "The suspense is killing me."

"Shut up," I said, smiling.

My gift came in a Chanel box, which was probably why Liza reached for it in the first place. I couldn't imagine this man had a Chanel bag lying around— and if he did, surely it was intended for another woman. Now, don't get me wrong, I would still accept it, but you get what I'm saying.

I opened the box—and found not luxury or jewelry, but something far more precious. A picture frame. Inside it, a photo of me and my mom.

But it was impossible. That picture never existed. It was her face from one photo, mine from another, blended seamlessly. We were standing side by side, smiling like we were that day at my high school graduation.

My breath caught. "How did you—"

"I took some pictures of you two separately and put them together," Evan said. "I wanted you to have the memory of her always being by your side."

The air shifted. Liza and Rashad went quiet. The laughter faded into something tender.

"This is the sweetest thing anybody's ever done for me," I whispered.

I threw my arms around him.

From somewhere behind us, Liza sighed dramatically. "Whew! I thought she got Chanel. Turns out I got the best gift after all. Cheers!"

That sent the tender moment into laughter.

87

CHAPTER 11

I worked alone in Evan's office, listening to R&B Christmas music. I paused and looked at the framed image of me and my mom. My heart melted. It was the picture I never got and always wanted.

I continued to work. My phone rang. It was Ryan on FaceTime.

"Merry Christmas, Ry," I said, so bright and bushy-tailed I almost didn't recognize my own voice.

Ryan was shirtless, wearing Christmas suspenders, antlers, and bells.

"Merry Christmas! Before things get crazy over here, I just want to make sure you saw the contract in your inbox. I sent it a couple of days ago and you didn't sign and send it back," he said—ever the professional.

I couldn't believe I had completely forgotten about that sketchy contract. I was so wrapped up in this foreign holiday cheer that I wasn't handling my business. That was not like me.

"Yeah, I read it and I don't know what to think," I said before Ryan cut me off.

"You don't know what to think? I'm sorry, am I speaking to Syndi Cole? Do you realize that Juke set this whole thing up—not only to be in your business but to try to control it?" Ryan emphasized.

"We do know that," he continued, moving away from the holiday noise until he found a quiet space. "Sydni, Juke could use this contract as leverage to take ownership of your company. He invested when you started and fed you clients."

"Which any partner would do," I replied.

"I can't believe I have to convince you of this," Ryan said. Then he stopped and looked at me. "You fell for the guy. You fell for the guy, didn't you?"

Not ready to profess my love and be the reason for my own downfall, I bossed up. "I got it from here, Ryan. I really appreciate you doing your due diligence."

"I'm just asking you not to be like those women who throw away everything they've worked so hard for over a man. I've done all I can do. Merry Christmas," Ryan said—and hung up.

He was right. I knew he was right. But I didn't want to have a conversation with Evan about Juke. It was early, and things were perfect. Evan was easily the most thoughtful man I'd ever been with. It wanted to keep peace between us.

I didn't know what to do. Ryan wanted me to speak up. Liza wanted me to keep quiet.

So I called Aunt Vi.

"Hey baby. How's it going up there? When ya coming home? You having a good Christmas?" she fired away.

"I am. Merry Christmas. Auntie, I need some advice," I prefaced.

"Okay," she said.

"I'll keep it short. I found out that Juke is an investor in Evan—the guy I'm helping's company—and I don't know if the guy is in on it or not. Juke could be using him to get some type of ownership of my company because she also gave me startup money. It's messy. I care about Evan," I said, talking fast.

"Oh, you *care* about Evan," she said, with raised eyebrows I could hear but not see.

"I do. And I care about Juke, but I don't know who to trust, and I don't know what to think," I told her as quietly as I could.

She paused.

"I don't know a lot about contracts and business," she said, "but I will say this—you can't be with a man you don't trust. You have to talk to him."

I thanked her, made sure everything at the house was good, and then prepared myself to confront Evan.

Rashad was spotting Evan on a bench press when I entered—on guard.

"Can I talk to Evan alone, please?" I said sternly.

It was alarming. The men shared a silent exchange, and Rashad left.

"Is everything alright?" Evan asked, concerned.

"No, everything is *not* alright," I said, holding up the contract. "You wanna tell me what this is?"

Evan took the papers and started reading. "This is a contract for my investors and your company. Did I miss something?"

"No. Apparently, I did." My voice was shaking now. "You're in business with my ex, Juke Matthews. You working for him? He sent me here to work with you so that he could continue to control me? Then you invite me and my friend here. All of this was set up?! This is sick!"

Evan's head was spinning. He tried to follow me but couldn't.

"I invited you to work. Your friend came because you showed up unprepared," he said, trying to recount the timeline of events.

"It was an honest mistake!"

"My investors thought I needed some help rebranding the company. This was not my idea," Evan said, trying to make sense of it all.

"So you take orders from Juke?" I asked.

"We have a board of investors—you know this. He's my neighbor; I met him in passing. We've had a few conversations that led to some business. I don't know him on a personal level. What is this? I'm on the chopping block?!"

"I don't even know what to say to you," I said. I believed Evan, but I didn't feel any better about the situation yet.

"What happened with my subscribers was not my fault," Evan said, devastated. "We aimed to present a space where people felt safe to find love. And I thought I was in a safe space to find it."

"You *were!* I wasn't," I fired back.

Liza entered. I could tell she was there to preserve the conversation but quickly realized it was too late.

"No, I'm caught up between something stupid with you and your ex—the ex that *'didn't do anything,'*" he said, regrouping. "You know, I trusted you. I thought it was safe to give. I didn't realize I was just another thing for you to fix."

Evan headed toward the door, but before he left, he turned back. "And now that you too have wasted my time and my money, your check will be in the mail."

He left.

I fought back tears. Liza hugged me tight enough to keep them in.

And then we got out of there.

CHAPTER 12

I stood in my pink silk pajamas and matching bonnet, staring at Juke from across my bedroom. The air between us was heavy—like all the words we'd both said before were floating around, just waiting for one of us to snatch them back.

He looked at me with those same tired eyes. "I thought I was doing a good thing," he said. "I promised you two things—to love you and to take care of you. I did that."

I shook my head slowly. "You didn't. You love me how you see fit to love me. But I need to be loved the way *I* want to be loved. I need security—the kind that doesn't come and go depending on your mood."

He exhaled hard, like I was exhausting him. "If I had proposed to you back then, it would've been pure manipulation. And now I'm ready. And that's not enough either? You want me to do it because I want to, or because you want me to?"

I didn't answer. He had a point—but the bigger point was why he wasn't ready after all this time. Would he ever be?

Later, I was in my office with Liza—my voice of reason or chaos, depending on the day. She was suspended across from me, one leg tucked under her, eyes lit with drama as I recounted the Juke visit.

"We want you to *want to* when we want you to," she said, pointing at me like she was preaching a sermon. "If I gotta tell you to do it—keep it!"

I screamed with the relief of validation, loud and full. "Exactly!"

Back home, Juke and I were still circling the same argument like another sad love song on repeat.

"That's not realistic!" he said, pacing. "What if you're just impatient?"

"Impatient?" I fired back. "You were just with another woman days ago. Are we just gonna skip over that part?"

He stopped. "That's how I know I wanna marry you! We ain't getting no younger. We might as well do it."

I couldn't help but hear Liza's voice echoing in my head, mocking him, mocking me. Both of us in exaggerated disbelief, like some sitcom laugh track was running in the background. *This man really just quoted Jagged Edge.* Those lyrics weren't good the first time we heard them! The song was just a bop, so we let it slide! You are not supposed to say that to anybody in real life!

"You're not in love with me," I told him. "You just don't wanna lose."

"Baby, listen to me—"

And then suddenly, he was on his knees. Both of them. His head rested against my stomach like he was praying to me.

"I love you," he said. "I'm sorry for everything I put you through. None of them meant anything to me."

I stared down at him. Unmoved because it felt familiar in the worst way. "You've said all of this before, Juke."

He shot up, voice rising. "Syd! I quit drinking! Didn't you see that? I did that for you."

I crossed my arms. "You should've done it so you could stop wrapping your car around trees."

Later, in the office again, Liza was sitting on the edge of her chair, practically foaming at the mouth. "You said that?" she whispered.

"I had to."

"What did he say?"

Back in my memory, I saw him—eyes wide, desperate. "Don't do this to us,

Syd. I heard you. I listened. I made changes. I stopped drinking. I'm playing better. I've been smarter with my money, started investing, poured it into your business."

And then he pulled out a red ring box.

My jaw hit the floor.

He opened it. "I'm not a perfect man. I just want to give you the life you deserve. If you'll have me."

I stared at him, at the ring, at everything that was supposed to mean *forever*.

In my office, Liza fell out of her chair. "Bitch, the ring so big it look like *you* won the championship!"

Back home, he kissed me. He slid the ring onto my finger. I grinned—half in disbelief, half in surrender. And then he took off my clothes. And baby… that was that.

Later, I was in my office again, staring at the ring glinting under the fluorescent lights. An eight-carat emerald-cut diamond in a split-shank platinum setting with pavé accents. It was alarming, elegant, and luxurious. And I deserved it.

Liza leaned back, satisfied, like she'd just finished a movie.

"Damn," she said.

"Right?"

"Absolutely."

I exhaled, heavy. "I got five years' time served."

She smirked. "This fool done came back a lot of times, but he ain't never came with a ring. What about Evan?"

I hesitated, dropping my head into my hands. "I miss him. I miss him so much."

"What are you gonna do?"

I walked to the window, arms folded across my chest. "What can I do? I'm engaged. Juke said everything I needed to hear. We're looking at houses. I refuse to go back to that penthouse, and I can't live down the street from Evan."

"Right," Liza said, though she didn't sound convinced.

"This is everything I ever wanted," I said, like if I said it enough, it would be true. "The time apart did him some good. Who wants that perfect love story anyway?"

Liza raised an eyebrow. "Yeah, except you actually have a perfect love story—with a man who didn't drag you."

I groaned. "I knowwwwwwww. I miss talking to Evan. I want to tell him about all this, but… he was right. Love takes time."

"Right," she repeated, but we both knew neither of us bought this shit.

"Well," she said finally, "you got him out of his mess. He didn't even need the gala. The media rollout you scheduled is already working."

She slid her iPad across the desk. I could barely keep up with the headlines.

"Not only that," she continued, "he did those interviews you set up. He admitted he's heartbroken. Members of his dating app are connecting to him on a new level. They made him a profile."

She handed me her phone. "Thousands of women are in his queue."

I laughed, hollow. "He's got thousands of women to choose from. He won't care about me getting back with Juke."

Liza looked me dead in the eyes. "You sure you wanna do this, Syd? If Evan sees you wearing that ring, you may never get him back."

And just like that, my chest caved in. Her words sank into me, slow and deep.

I stared at the ring on my finger—shining, heavy, wrong.

All I could think was: I'd been launched into something I might not come back from. And this time, Juke was the *bird in the hand.*

CHAPTER 13

I sat at a small table tucked into the corner of a quiet restaurant—the kind of place with dim lighting, cloth napkins, and too many forks. The kind of restaurant where they ask a couple of times if it's "just one."

The stem of my wine glass caught the glow from a candle, and I traced the rim with my finger, pretending I wasn't waiting.

I'd dressed up more than I needed to—a little black dress, a roller set pinned into a soft French roll, a stained lip liner with pink gloss. I wasn't trying *not* to look how I felt.

I looked down at my eight-carat emerald solitaire. It was astounding, especially with the lighting that elevated its clarity. I had wanted this ring for so many years, and it didn't feel like I thought it would feel.

A waiter glided over with a bottle of Cabernet, the cork already loosened, and I smiled politely as he poured, masking my feelings. I was halfway through admiring the color—deep ruby, like velvet—when I saw movement through the window.

Liza.

She was outside, walking her dog, light on her feet, the leash taut in her hand. Our eyes met for half a second, and her face flashed with surprise—then recognition. Her mouth opened, a smile forming, and before I could even react, she was waving and heading for the door.

My stomach sank.

By the time she stepped inside, Rashad had arrived, sliding into the seat across from me with that easy grin of his. He always moved like he owned the air around him.

"Sydni," he said, settling in. "You picked the place well."

I smiled, ignoring the knot in my chest. I didn't want to turn around, didn't want to see Liza's face when she realized I wasn't dining alone. But I caught the faintest reflection in the window—her frozen expression, the confusion, then the flash of hurt.

He hugged me like a brother, and when he took his seat, she was gone.

I swallowed hard and lifted the wine glass to my lips, pretending not to notice. I didn't want to ruin the night for him. And I already knew I'd have to have a conversation with her. No sense in making a scene and having it now.

Rashad tilted his glass and swirled the Cabernet, trying to look like he knew what he was doing. "This one's kind of bitter, isn't it?"

I smiled gingerly. "It's not bitter. It's dry."

He blinked at me, brow furrowing. "Dry?"

"It's a Cabernet. And cabs are reliable," I said, leaning forward a little. "It has hints of blackcurrant, blackberry, cedar, tobacco, green bell pepper… sometimes even mint. It's an acquired taste. Try it."

He took a sip, and I watched his expression change—that little spark of discovery. "I can taste the berries!"

I chuckled. "Exactly."

As he reached for the bottle again, I subtly turned the diamond on my finger inward, the massive stone hidden against my palm. The ring felt heavy— suddenly too bright for the moment. I didn't want to spark a conversation about it, and I certainly didn't want it to get back to Evan.

"Liza's favorite," I said, maybe too casually, "is a blend of all of these. It's called *Prisoner*."

Rashad laughed. "*Prisoner?* People go to prison over wine?"

I smiled, though something in me twisted. "I honestly don't know why they call it that. But it's bold—tastes like rich blackberry, cherry, dark chocolate, fig, roasted coffee, and spice."

He tried it, eyes closing for a second as he savored it. "Mmm. That's good."

I grinned, but my thoughts were elsewhere—on Evan, on Juke, out on the street, wondering where Liza had gone, and what she'd seen in those few silent seconds.

The truth was, I missed Evan so much. Getting a ring from Juke was validating, and that felt good too—but I just missed talking to Evan.

And just when my anxiety was about to get the best of me, Rashad tried another wine—and enjoyed it.

The hum of the office was the only sound—the low electric buzz from the computer, the faint rattle of the air vent overhead. I'd been staring at the same spreadsheet for fifteen minutes, typing nonsense just to make it look like progress.

My mind was everywhere but here, and the voices inside it were loud, searching for solid ground to latch onto.

I sank deeper into my chair and rubbed my temples. The screen blurred. It wasn't the work that was exhausting—it was pretending I cared about it right now.

Finally, I gave up and reached for the remote. The small TV in the corner blinked to life, lighting the office in a soft blue glow. *The Preacher's Wife* was on—Whitney Houston smiling that angelic smile. I let it play. The music, the warmth of it, helped me feel less alone.

Then the door opened.

"Hey, baby."

I flinched.

Juke stood in the doorway, grinning like he'd just stepped into a surprise party instead of my workspace.

"Hey," I said, forcing my voice into something that sounded light, sweet. Fake as hell.

Before I could even stand, he leaned down and kissed me—long, possessive. I tried to pull away, but he held me there, deepening it until I had to laugh awkwardly just to break the tension.

"What's up?" I asked, straightening my blouse like that might restore some distance between us.

"I went to pick you up," he said, smiling wide. "Surprise you. Auntie said you were still at the office, so I figured—why not come by, take you shopping? Everything's on sale."

He laughed like this was the most romantic thing in the world. I forced a small laugh back.

"I'm working, baby," I said softly, returning to my desk—my barricade.

His eyes drifted past me to the TV. "Looks like you're watching a movie."

"It helps me think," I lied.

"Baby, you think too much," he said, sliding closer. "You don't need this company anymore. You got me."

He leaned in for another kiss. I let him have a quick peck, then turned my head away, pretending to refocus on my laptop.

When I looked back, he was staring at me, his brow furrowed.

"What's up, Syd?" he asked quietly.

"Nothing," I said too quickly.

He leaned back in the seat across from me, fully taking me in. He nodded toward my hand. "You got your ring on the wrong finger."

My stomach twisted. I looked down. Damn. I'd forgotten.

"Oh," I murmured, fumbling to take it off. "Yeah… you know, when you gave it to me—"

"*Gave* it to you?" he cut in, eyes narrowing. "I proposed to you. Marriage. You're my woman. Soon to be my wife. And I think it's about time we set a date."

"A wedding," I echoed almost out of breath. The walls closing in like they tend to do.

"We can go to the courthouse today if you want to," Juke said nonchalantly.

I closed my eyes for a moment, breathing slowly so it wouldn't turn into an argument. "Baby," I said softly, "it doesn't fit my ring finger. It means a lot to me, and I didn't want to lose it."

I held the ring out to him like an offering. He was still tense, his jaw working.

"You just want me to get it sized?" he asked finally.

"Yeah."

"Okay," he said, standing abruptly. "Well, let's go to the store now."

He turned toward the door, expecting me to follow.

"I'm gonna stay here," I said, forcing a smile. "I still have work to do."

He stopped, turned halfway back. "You sure everything's okay?"

I stood and kissed him—quick, reassuring. "Yeah. And thank you… for understanding," I said, to end the conversation.

His shoulders relaxed. That boyish grin returned.

"You know," he said, touching my chin, "you're the best thing I ever *won*."

Won.

He left, pleased with himself, whistling down the hallway.

The door clicked shut behind him, and I just stood there—frozen, disgusted, relieved.

I turned off the TV. The room fell silent again.

For a moment, I just stared at the empty doorway, thinking about the word *won*, how it clanged in my chest like a warning bell.

And then, quietly, inevitably, my thoughts drifted back to Evan.

CHAPTER 14

Sugar cookies and pine aromas collided to fill up the YMCA rec center. Kid-made paper snowflakes hung from the ceiling, and tinsel shimmered from every folding chair and corner. Christmas might've been behind us technically but the spirit was still alive and well.

The girls sat in a half circle, their faces lit up like Christmas lights—giggles, whispers, and nervous excitement everywhere.

I sat among them—between three of the girls—with Liza across the circle. She wouldn't even look at me. Every time I tried to catch her eye, she focused harder on wrapping ribbon around a candy cane or straightening one of the kids' bows. The space between us felt heavier than it should have in a room full of holiday cheer.

It had been a couple of days since she saw me with Rashad, and this had truly gone on too long. I also didn't recognize my life. How was I not talking to Liza or Evan and *engaged* to Juke? At least I didn't have to wear the ring while he got it sized. I had no intention of taking it back—but I was gonna deal with that later.

Aunt Vi sat a few tables ahead, wrapping gifts with a small army of older ladies. Their laughter and gossip mixed with the sound of tape ripping and paper crinkling. For a moment, it almost felt normal.

Then Cadence stood. Eleven years old, tiny voice, big heart—the kind of kid who still believed in magic even if the world had given her too many reasons not to.

"I don't really care about getting adopted anymore," she said. Her voice trembled a little, but she held her chin high. "You guys are my family already. I just want someone to believe in me."

The words hit me square in the chest.

I could feel my throat close up, that hot, sudden sting behind my eyes. Because I knew what that felt like—to want someone to *see* you, not just your good parts, but your cracks too. To want someone to believe in you when you don't even believe in yourself.

Evan believed in me. That's what gutted me.

The girls clapped, cheering for Cadence as she smiled shyly and sank into a sea of hugs. I clapped too, forcing my hands together, pretending my heart wasn't breaking in the middle of a Christmas party.

Later, after the gifts had been opened and the girls were squealing over dolls and board games, I found myself sweeping up wrapping paper beside Aunt Vi.

She didn't even look up when she said it. "Imagine that. A newly engaged woman in public without her ring."

I threw my hands in the air. "Excuse me—what?"

"When I got engaged," she said, still folding a piece of discarded tissue paper like it was gold, "I would make a U-turn on three wheels if I left the house without mine."

"I gave it back," I said quietly.

That made her look up. "Does Juke know that?"

"I told him it needed to be sized." I sighed, setting the broom against the table. "Auntie, I can't marry him. I think he made me wait so long just to make me feel like I had to earn it—like I had to prove I was good enough to marry. And now I…"

My voice cracked. Tears started before I could stop them.

Aunt Vi didn't hesitate. She grabbed me by the arm and pulled me in close, whispering fiercely, "Pull it together. This is a community event, baby. These girls got it hard enough. They don't need to see you fall apart too."

I sucked in a deep breath and swallowed it all down.

She softened a little. "Juke'll do better with the truth," she said. "Just tell him. And Liza told me you got feelings for that man you was working for."

I threw my hands up again. "Excuse me—what?"

"Don't get mad over Liza telling your business," she said, eyes cutting through me. "The bigger issue is you found someone you care about. That's all."

I couldn't hold it in anymore. "Auntie, he's the sweetest man," I said, voice trembling. "He thinks I'm so smart and so funny. He's thoughtful. I feel like I could believe every word he says."

Aunt Vi smirked. "Now don't get crazy. He's still a man."

I laughed through my tears, wiping my face.

Then the laughter faded, and the truth slipped out before I could catch it. "I didn't just break Evan's trust," I said. "I broke my own rules. I finally let someone see the softest part of me… and I still got played."

"You didn't get played," she said. "You young people are so worried about getting your feelings hurt. Nobody ever died from that. Feelings get hurt. That's part of living."

"I don't want my feelings hurt," I muttered.

"Well then sit in a box," she said dryly. "See how you like that life."

I laughed again.

"Prioritize the love," she said, wagging her finger. "Not avoiding getting hurt."

I thought about that. Really thought about it. "I don't know what to do to fix it," I whispered. "I'm a fixer. I fix things. That's what I do."

"Maybe this time," she said, "you stop hiding behind control. Try letting somebody love you without it."

"I don't need to control things. I just be trying to make sure things go the right way," I said. I heard the words when they fell out of my mouth. Aunt Vi caught me catching myself.

"Real love doesn't need your strength," Aunt Vi replied. "Real love needs you to let go."

She left me standing there with that truth hanging heavy in the air.

I wanted to sit with it, but of course, Liza picked that exact moment to show up—clutching her iPad like it was a live grenade.

"I don't even know why I'm trying to help you," she said, "but Kesha is reporting about you on her podcast. Today, you're the tea."

I blinked. "Be so fucking for real."

She rolled her eyes. "Do I look like I'm kidding?"

I reached for the iPad, and there she was—Kesha—in her studio, mic on, hair perfect, talking into the camera like she was delivering gospel.

And just like that, whatever was left of my quiet moment of reflection vanished.

Because now, apparently, I was the story.

Liza pouted next to me in the backseat of a Suburban.

"Can we just talk about this and move past it? You're not gonna stop being my friend," I said.

"Who says we're friends?" Liza replied.

It stung, and she knew it.

"Friends don't go out with each other's mans behind their back."

"Liza—"

"Don't try to clean it up now," she cut me off. "I've done nothing but support you my entire life, and as soon as I meet someone I like, you gotta go out with him? That's foul, Syd."

I was hurt, but I swallowed it.

"He told me you invited him to dinner. He knows you drink wine and he's not a big wine drinker. He wanted me to point him in the direction of your favorite wine so he could gift you with a nice bottle," I told her.

Tears welled in Liza's eyes.

"I'm sorry, Sydni," she said. "I should've known better. I thought—"

"Rashad cares about you. And I would never do anything like that to you," I said gently.

Liza exhaled and leaned on my shoulder.

"I'm really sorry," she whispered.

My phone rang. It was Juke. Liza saw it.

"Before you answer that," she said, "I think you should know that they exchanged words."

"Evan and Juke had a conversation about me and you're just now telling me?" I asked, terrified.

Juke called again. I ended it without beginning it.

"It just happened yesterday," Liza continued. "Rashad told me about it. Said it was wild—like one of those scenes in those boardroom movies you love, except *you* were on the chopping block, bitch."

I didn't want to hear it. But of course, I had to.

Rashad had been so pissed about the whole thing when he told it to me, I could almost see it playing out.

So *Bird in the Hand*, Evan's app, was having a meeting with their board of directors. The room was full of investors. Some of them were already thinking of pulling out of the company because of what was going on, and they wanted an update—how it went working with me, could it be saved, blahzay blahzay.

Juke was there too, sitting all puffed up in his suit like he belonged.

Rachel—the woman running the meeting—was sharp and polished, the kind of woman who could turn a *yes* into a *no* just by how she raised her eyebrow. She started talking about timelines, execution, the usual corporate gospel.

Then Evan cut her off.

"The gala's cancelled," he said.

Just like that.

Rashad told me the silence that followed was thick enough to choke on. Rachel blinked, the investors started whispering, and then she asked, trying to keep her tone smooth, "Was there a problem with Ms. Cole?"

When Rashad said Evan didn't even flinch, my stomach dropped.

"Not at all. She's phenomenal with what she does," Evan said. "But I'm not going to continue working with her."

And that's when Juke spoke up—of course he did—leaning back in his chair like he owned the place.

"And why is that?"

According to Rashad, Evan turned his head slowly, met Juke's eyes, and said nothing. Just looked at him. That kind of look that says more than a paragraph ever could.

Rashad said he could feel the air shift in the room. He'd even stood up, ready to step in, but Evan just gave him a small nod—the kind that said *I've got this*.

"I don't owe anyone an explanation," Evan finally said, putting his foot down and standing on business.

Rachel, being who she is, decided that was the end of it. She adjourned the meeting, packed her notes, and left the room, her heels clicking sharp against the tile. Everyone followed—except Juke.

That's when it really went left.

Rashad said Juke stayed behind, pretending to play it cool. "Hey, man," he said to Evan, "I meant no disrespect. Sydni's my fiancée. I try not to mix business with pleasure but—"

And Evan stopped him.

"She's what?"

That's when my heart skipped. Not a face-off between the two men I loved.

Rashad said the tension in the room changed completely—like the air had turned electric.

Juke repeated himself, a little more defensive this time. "My fiancée."

Evan just looked at him and said, "You sure about that?"

Rashad said Juke's face dropped. Like he'd suddenly realized Evan wasn't the man he'd sent to handle business—he was a threat now.

"Yo," Juke said, "you got something you need to tell me?"

Evan didn't hesitate. "Yeah. You're no longer needed on the board."

Rashad swore Juke almost jumped out of his seat. "What you say?!"

He had to step between them—said he put a hand on Juke's shoulder, but Juke shook it off like a bull ready to charge.

Then Juke said something that made my skin crawl even hearing it secondhand:

"Oh, okay. You caught a few feelings for Syd. That's understandable. She's an amazing woman. But the thing about me is, I don't lose. Sydni is mine."

And Evan just looked him dead in the eye and said, calm as stone, "Seemed kinda single last time I saw her."

When Liza repeated that line to me, I swear my heart just about jumped out of my chest.

According to Rashad, they were standing so close by then that you could've fit a knife between them and hit both.

Juke's voice went low, dangerous. "I sent you there to do a job."

And Evan—God bless him—didn't blink. "You ain't send me nowhere to do a mothafuckin' thing. I'm a man. This isn't the field, Juke," he said. "This is business. This is *my* domain."

Rashad said the heat coming off Juke was something else, like he was about to tackle him right there in the conference room. Rashad had to step in again, put himself between them, tell Juke to take a walk.

Juke eventually did.

But Rashad said when he left, the way he looked back at Evan—it wasn't over. Not by a long shot.

When Liza finished the story, I just sat there in silence. My heart was pounding, my hands shaking a little.

Because even though I hadn't been in that room, I could *feel* it. Every word, every look, every unspoken truth hovering in the air between those two men.

I knew I needed to officially break things off with Juke as soon as possible.

But it still had to wait—because we were pulling up to Késha's studio.

Késha sat on her pink couch, looking like a doll in a dollhouse — complete with a platinum blonde updo. We had caught her mid-take.

"We just got a tip that Sydni Cole, the brand architect behind some of your favorite figures (including yours truly)," Késha said, illustrating her own coke-bottle shape in the air with her hands, "is under fire. Now, I know Sydni personally, but y'all know that's not gonna stop me from giving y'all the tea."

"Well, that didn't take long," I said to Liza.

"I told you," Liza replied.

"The tea is: Juke Matthews is the bank behind Sydni's thriving business. The pair is engaged, and that blew up in her face when Sydni decided to link up with one of her clients. That's right. She cheated on Juke," Liza continued. I started to walk up on stage, but Liza held me back.

Késha continued, "Turns out Sydni isn't using the baby train to get ahead like most of you. She's playing the men against each other, using her business as a weapon."

I had heard enough. I busted on her set, shocking the hell out of Késha. Once bold, now scared.

"Whoa. It's just entertainment," Késha said, looking for one of her people to step in and save her.

"You think you got something on me?" I asked Késha as I sat down on her couch. "I've built my brand on perfection. But real connection is messy. I'm not a fixer. I'm a builder. Starting with me. You cannot shame me into silence. So let's air this thing out!"

"So when you were hired to work on Evan Sterling's company, you weren't aware that your fiancé, Juke Matthews, hired him?" Késha asked.

"Not at all. And I'm not going to marry Juke," I said, then turned to the camera. "I'm sorry, Juke. This is not how I intended on things playing out. This is messed up, but people love to stay in other people's business."

"Was that an exclusive?" Késha got excited, not caring about the shade.

"This is not about you. Or your show. This is my life. Working with Evan was not a scheme to get me to the top. I care about both of them," I said, setting the record straight.

"Yes, roster," Késha said as she sipped her tea. I took her tea from her mouth.

"Do not sip your tea on that. This is not tea," I said, trying to regain control. "I'll say this — I was like a lot of people. I was so busy looking over my shoulder that I couldn't see that what was perfect for me was right in front of me."

I looked over at Liza, and she was watching me proudly.

"Evan," Késha said, committed to getting the scoop.

"Yeah. Evan. But I won't keep performing control to avoid accountability. Starting now, I'm rebuilding in truth. Juke Matthews is not my man. There is no scenario where we are getting back together. He has helped me over the years but he is not responsible for my success of my company. My team and I work tirelessly for our clients everyday."

"So Juke is a free agent, ladies. And what about you and Evan?" Késha pried.

"I can't tell you something I don't know. But when I do, I won't. Keep my name out of your mouth. And you are no longer my client. My rebrand doesn't include mess, and that's all you ever were," I said to Késha pointedly.

I un-mic'd and left with Liza leaving Késha stunned.

CHAPTER 15

I walked through my office and packed things up. I took branding pieces off the walls and boxed everything up. I had helped so many people get their fresh start — and now it was time for me to get one of my own. And I felt damn good about it. I could see Ryan in the conference room doing the same.

Liza came in chipper, light on her feet, sipping a latte.

"It was just like I always imagined it, Syd. I opened the door, and there was Rashad. I hung his coat on the empty hook next to mine. He presented me with a bottle of red wine — a good bottle! Thank you so much for helping him," Liza said, excited.

I wasn't really in the mood. I was happy for my girl, but I had professed my love for Evan in front of the world, dumped Juke, and I still hadn't heard from Evan. Not even a text. Maybe he felt nothing. Maybe I made it all up.

"He sits at the table in his seat, and I pour us both a glass of wine, and then we cheers and eat dinner," Liza continued. "It happened just like I saw it in my head. I can't believe it. I had to pinch myself several times that night. Syd, I have wanted this for so long. I played this out at night so many times. And then it happened. It really happened," Liza said, with tears in her eyes.

I hugged her and cried with her. Dreams be coming true.

Once all of the old branding was off the walls, the three of us hung a new placard that said **"Cole Standard."** I stood back and looked at it proudly.

"You know I love a rebrand," I told them. "I emailed you guys the list of clients we will no longer be working with. It's time to clear the mess everywhere. Money is not enough to get us on your team. They need purpose."

"I'm here for that! And that podcast stunt was genius. The inquiries are flooding in," Ryan added.

"Maybe it's time to hire and train some new agents," Liza said.

"Nah, that's not what I see. I see the opportunity to keep the same team and raise the price," I said with intention.

"I like that! You wanna hunker down and get started this evening?" Ryan asked, practically grabbing his laptop.

I thought, stopped, and smiled for a minute.

"Actually, no. I'm going to take New Year's Eve off with my family and friends," I said, resolved.

"Sydni Cole is taking a holiday off! Now *that* is a rebrand," Liza said excitedly.

"You don't gotta tell me twice! Are we done here? I wanna grab party hats for the crab boil," Ryan asked as he walked out the door.

"Yeah, we're good. See ya… soon," I laughed at his absence. He was gone before I could finish my sentence.

"Hey, I wanted to see if it was okay if I brought Rashad?" Liza asked gingerly.

"Of course. I'm not her, and this ain't that. Don't ever be scared to be happy in front of me," I said.

Liza left too.

I looked up at my own rebrand, satisfied.

CHAPTER 16

Suddenly, it was New Year's Eve. The party was in full swing with people of all ages. Couples danced to Luther Vandross's upbeat songs, and children ran through the house. People ate crabs, sides, and drank merrily. I tried not to completely lose my shit while people enjoyed themselves in my house.

Aunt Vi threw this party every year, but this was the first year I was back living here while she did it. Usually, I popped in with Juke and popped out before it got too rowdy.

Aunt Vi prepped a fresh batch of crabs. I helped her bring them out of the boiling water without making a mess. Liza and Rashad arrived holding hands and carrying Tupperware.

"I brought sausages, corn, peanuts, and eggs to add to the boil," Liza said.

"That's just perfect. Hand it here. Oh, and who is this?" Aunt Vi said. She couldn't wait.

Liza beamed. "This is Rashad, my boyfriend." She presented him like he was Hercules. "And this is Aunt Vi — and you know Syd."

Rashad leaned in to hug me and Aunt Vi.

"It's really nice to meet you," he told Aunt Vi. She went to blushing like he'd asked for her phone number.

"Happy New Year! Glad you could make it," I told Rashad as I grabbed more food from the refrigerator.

"Liza said it was a party, so I hope it's not a problem that I brought—" Rashad started.

Evan arrived — in what felt like slow motion. I breathed deep, heart melting. Aunt Vi caught the tray of food in my hand before I dropped it.

"You look better in person than on the computer," Aunt Vi said without her own permission.

Liza grabbed her, and Rashad took off with them, leaving me and Evan alone.

"Hi," he said tenderly.

"Hi," I replied.

"I hope it's okay that I—" he started.

"Yes, of course. I'm glad you're here," I assured him.

"Okay, cool," he said. He took in the space and found his way back to me. "You look nice."

"Thank you. So do you," I told him. I was so freaking glad he came.

"I didn't want to show up empty-handed, so I brought these," Evan said. I hadn't even realized he was holding anything until he handed it over — a plate of flat sweet potato biscuits. I looked at them. They looked terrible. We both laughed.

"I missed you so much, Syd. I overreacted. Then I heard you were engaged and, I don't know. I didn't know what to think. But I'm sorry for my part in all of it," Evan explained.

"I missed you so much too. I'm not with him. I don't want to be with him. I'm sorry too. For everything."

"I saw the podcast. He's no longer an investor in my—" Evan continued.

"It's okay if he is," I said.

"He's not. You made me realize something, Syd. I was scared. I was scared to love, scared to open up. The time, the money — it's nothing without you."

I felt so relieved to hear him say that. I hugged him long and strong. Evan bent over to whisper in my ear, "We are doing this."

"This is the only thing worth doing."

Evan pulled a slim jewelry box out of his jacket pocket. My eyes lit up. He told me to open it. When I did, I pulled out a charm bracelet with a box, a ladder, a horse, and an umbrella.

"Because you ground me, you're my family, you're my friend. Sometimes you're gonna be my storm, but you're also the reason I climb," he said. "You're my horse. My ladder's nothing without you tied to it."

I melted. I was putty in this man's hands. This was the moment I'd waited for my whole life — for a man to love me like I love. He kissed me passionately.

Liza and Aunt Vi watched me surrender proudly. In a room full of champagne, Rashad brought Liza a glass of wine, and the countdown into the next chapter of our lives began.

"Five, four, three, two, one! Happy! New! Year!"

EPILOGUE

A year later

The wind whipped my weave as I stepped onto the sidewalk, the chill biting but familiar. Christmas time again — but everything felt different this year, lighter somehow. My style was simpler now, softer. Loose curls brushed my shoulders; my makeup was minimal, my outfit relaxed but still me. New, but still Sydni.

As I walked past the billboards lining the street, I caught glimpses of myself smiling back — Evan's arms wrapped around me from behind in each one. *An app that gets out of the way of love.* The tagline still made me grin. We had actually pulled it off.

When I reached my office, the familiar hum of the building greeted me. My new branding peeked out in subtle places — the logo on the glass door, the muted palette on the walls. I sank into my chair and glanced at the photo Evan had given me last Christmas: Mom, laughing, frozen in time. Next to it sat a picture of me and Evan, one from the day we got engaged. My ring caught the light as I adjusted the frame — a quiet, happy reminder. A gentle relief to be out of those streets for good.

I pressed the intercom button on my phone.
"Can I pull you guys for a chat?"

A moment later, Liza waddled in — well, not *waddled*, but moved with that unmistakable grace of someone very pregnant. Her left hand rested instinctively on her belly, her wedding rings glinting. Ryan followed, notebook in hand, already ready. They settled into the seats across from me.

"I think it's time," I said.

Ryan looked up, eyes bright. "We love a rebrand!"

"It's not a full rebrand," I told him, smiling. "It's more of a distinction. We don't just build brands anymore. We build wholeness."

"I like wholeness," Liza said, leaning forward.

Ryan scribbled something down. I glanced at my charm bracelet, tracing the small heart-shaped piece with my thumb.

"Yeah," I murmured. "Soft. Whole. Loved."

"Cool. Shall I order food and we hunker down and get started?" Ryan said, ready to go.

Just then, there was a knock on the door. Evan peeked in, grinning. "You two ready? We can get to Jersey in an hour if we leave now."

I laughed, leaning back in my chair. "No, Ryan. I think I'm gonna take the rest of the year off — spend time with my friends and family."

"That's my cue!" Ryan said, snapping his notebook shut.

We all laughed as we gathered our things. Through the window, I caught sight of a horse-drawn carriage passing by — two people bundled together, laughing, their breath turning to mist in the cold air.

Evan held the door for Liza and me, his hand brushing mine as we stepped outside. He took the passenger seat beside Rashad, who was already grinning behind the wheel. As the car pulled away, I glanced back once at the office — its windows glowing warm against the December dusk.

Another year ending.
A new one just beginning.

ABOUT THE AUTHOR

TIFFANY BLACK is an actress, screenwriter, producer, and multidisciplinary artist whose work bridges beauty, storytelling, and soul. A graduate of Florida State University and Cornell University, Tiffany brings depth and dimension to every project she touches—on screen, on the page, and beyond. Her performances (*Love Is__*, *P-Valley*, *Mona Lisa and the Blood Moon*) and her acclaimed digital presence have made her a voice of ambition, reinvention, and millennial Black womanhood. With *This Christmas in Love*, Tiffany Black delivers a luminous debut—a story about friendship, faith, and the kind of love that finds you when you finally believe you deserve it.